No Balloons
Robert Zola Christensen

translated from the Danish

by Nina Sokol

Spuyten Duyvil
New York City

Sincere appreciation to The Danish Arts Foundation for their financial support towards the translation of this book.

THE DANISH ARTS FOUNDATION

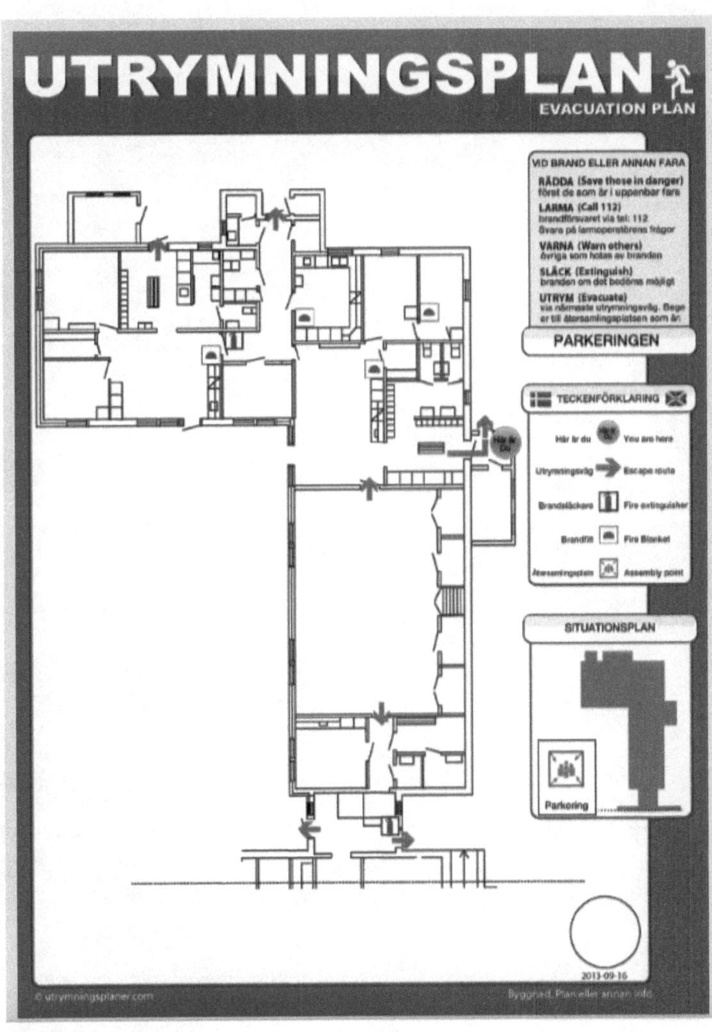

UTRYMNINGSPLAN
EVACUATION PLAN

VID BRAND ELLER ANNAN FARA
RÄDDA (Save those in danger)
först de som är i uppenbar fara
LARMA (Call 112)
brandförsvaret via tel: 112
Svara på larmoperatörens frågor
VARNA (Warn others)
övriga som hotas av branden
SLÄCK (Extinguish)
branden om det bedöms möjligt
UTRYM (Evacuate)
via närmaste utrymningsväg. Bege
er till återsamlingsplatsen som är:
PARKERINGEN

TECKENFÖRKLARING
Här är du — You are here
Utrymningsväg — Escape route
Brandsläckare — Fire extinguisher
Brandfilt — Fire Blanket
Återsamlingsplats — Assembly point

SITUATIONSPLAN
Parkering

2013-09-16
© utrymningsplaner.com
Byggnad, Plan eller annan info.

1

The lights turn on as I enter the room

and I throw my bag on the floor and start searching the shelves for Olga's paper. It's crazy that I haven't yet managed to get just a little bit more organized. For a while I would make two-three copies of certain documents in order to increase my chances of finding them whenever I was forced to search for them, like I am now.

She'll be here in less than five minutes. Where the hell is it? Annika's parents are coming over for dinner. She's really looking forward to it because we'll be planning her 40th birthday party coming up in mid-June and she really loves her birthdays.

I can hear David Håkonsson on the other side of the wall. There's a completely different kind of order in there. But that's mostly because he never makes any real effort. He sees himself as a handball player. He is a timetabler and administrator but waiting for his big breakthrough in professional handball, which is never going to happen. Nonetheless, every time we meet to set up the exam schedule, which we do a few times a month, I am forced to listen to funny stories from the world of handball that aren't in the least bit funny. I'm pretty fed up with it, so that's why I've started settling matters via email even though we're only sitting two meters away from each other. I can tell that he's puzzled by this when we meet in the hallway, but that's just the way it'll have to be.

There's that damn paper. Stuck between Foucault's "Les mots et les choses" and a stack of evaluations from intro class, spring semester 2012 or "vårterminen" as they say here in Sweden.

I sit down in my chair and skim through the paper. She wrote to me three days ago asking if she could come pick it up and get some feedback. "Sure, you can," I answered, but what can she possibly expect to gain by it? She handed in the paper four months ago.

I see a number of careless mistakes now. On the cover page there's a historical map of Denmark from back when there really was a Denmark to speak of, and the place where we are now was a part of Danish territory. Olga Preobraznenskaya is her full name. Preobraznenskaya.

I remember her, too. She always sat way up front in class, high cheekbones, pale. If I recall correctly she also once said that she came from St. Petersburg and here she is, Olga Preobra-snenskaya-something-or-other, in real life. Hello I say, getting up and inviting her into the office. She is taller than I remember. at least 175. Very slender with a delicate build. You've got to give her that.

I'm glad you had time, she says, smiling with her scarlet mouth. She insists on speaking Danish even though she struggles with the pronunciation of my softer language. Her Swedish isn't anything to write home about either but then again you hear a little bit of everything spoken here at the Centre for Languages and Literature. We're truly tolerant.

I slap the flat of my hand down on the paper as though to say, "So, what do we have here? What is it you'd like to know?

She doesn't answer but starts unbuttoning her cardigan with those long fingers of hers. Underneath she is wearing a white top with two thin straps. I can see it all very clearly, the two very small, well, yes…little girl breasts. She is not wearing a bra.

I randomly turn the pages of the paper and say something about the Roskilde Pact, all the while staring at what she apparently wants to show me.

Then she says, in a Danish which she manages to mangle so badly that it's practically incomprehensible, that the reason why she wanted to see me was to ask me whether I would be her supervisor for her Masters thesis which she plans to start working on in the fall. She had actually been thinking of expanding on the paper I have in my hands and that's why she came to see me.

I tell her that it is certainly a relevant and interesting topic, no doubt about that, but that she has to remember that my area of expertise is Danish literature and ethnography. I point toward some signs hanging on my bulletin board and explain that I have spent February and March running around all over Denmark and Sweden taking pictures of signs because the signs we use, as for example road signs, say a lot about the spaces of consciousness in which they are put up. As an illustrative example I point out the fact that where we in Denmark have signs that say, "The dog bites," the Swedish version, which is a tad bit more cautious, reads, "Beware of the dog." And what does that indicate in terms of who we are and how we think?

She smiles in a way that makes me realize that I've gotten too carried away.

Which, naturally, makes me angry because who does she think she's dealing with anyway? That trick might work back home in Russia but she has no business coming here and playing on a womanhood that isn't even there, and, as I catch myself staring without shame at her little gum drops, I hear myself say that the Danish Language Department here at Lund University covers, of course, a vast variety of subjects and that I'll think about it.

I like that idea a lot

I say and take a sip of the white wine that my father-in-law has brought with him. He's a bit of a connoisseur.

We're standing out on the new terrace. He tells me that the apple trees I just recently planted actually aren't apple trees but quinces. They're inedible, he says. Not even the birds eat them. He tells me that the only thing I'll get out of that tree is a hell of a lot of windfalls in the autumn which won't be worth jack shit.

That's the story of my life, I say and we laugh at that a little. And drink more wine.

I like him, my father-in-law. He's a former high school teacher and he takes most things in stride.

My mother-in-law, on the other hand, I can't stand. It's become increasingly clear that she has never thought that I was the one Annika should have chosen. And she's afraid of everything.

Yes, I like that idea a lot, I say once more as we stand at the door and my in-laws are finally on their way home. We've decided that Annika will celebrate her birthday in Simrishamn on June 18th. It will only include close family members and a few girlfriends. Maybe a few colleagues can come too, but that'll be it.

After they leave and Annika is watching Skavlan on TV I go upstairs and sit down in front of my computer. I know that she hates when I do that, but I don't want to watch Skavlan. He's self-absorbed but trying to come across as humble. He doesn't pull it off very well.

There's an email from Olga. She thanks me for the meeting today and then she asks whether I've had time to think about it. I sense another sting of anger and I picture her as she sat there with her skinny body, legs and bones sticking out everywhere, no breasts in sight. I answer her that right now it looks like I'll be able to take on her thesis.

When on the following Wednesday I

walk through the cafeteria carrying a cup of steaming hot coffee in my hand as I make my way to the Faculty Club for an LK1 meeting I catch sight of Olga.

She and a guy are standing very close to one another in the rain. It's pouring down in torrents. I can see that she's explaining something to him that is painful. He resembles a fair-haired Torsten whom I once had as a student. The kind of guy who's spoiled and has chubby cheeks and will resemble a boy for most of his life.

There are many Swedish men, incidentally, who look like that. Bjørn Borg is one of them and frankly I think that the whole thing started with him.

Olga lights a cigarette even though there's a sign, and a big one at that, indicating that smoking is only allowed at a distance of at least 15 meters from the building.

Which, in this case, is a good distance out in the rain. But apparently such things don't concern Olga. I'm not sure whether I like her. But she looks fantastic, you can't get around that. She has something magnetic about her which I can't quite put my finger on. I think it has to do with her long limbs. Her legs are long, her arms are long--even her fingers are longer than usual, and I like it all. Also the expression in her eyes. She has a certain radiance about her that is both raw and Russian and yet at the same time is mixed with a sense of insecurity that is probably something you see in most young people. It's very sexy.

Through the glass door to the Faculty Club I see Britta waving me over. The meeting is about to begin.

I walk slowly so as not to miss anything, which I don't because Torsten is now slinking away with his head lowered. Out in the rain you go, Torsten, yes, out in the rain with you, buddy.

I pick up the pace as I make my way to the meeting which I know is going to be nothing but a sleep-inducing complete waste of time, but I also know that it won't be long before I see Olga again. She is scheduled for her first supervision meeting with me in two hours.

I stand looking down the hallway

because Olga should have been here 15 minutes ago. This is just unacceptable. I go back inside my office and put on my raincoat because it's still raining. No, actually, it's pissing down. When she arrives in just a moment I'll have left for the day because I refuse to waste my time waiting for her all day like an idiot. I'm not the kind of guy who waits and I'm certainly not the kind of guy to waste my time.

I hear rapid footsteps out in the hallway.

I sit down and try to look focused. The rain coat. I realize I'm still wearing it. I quickly tear it off and place it on the table. That won't work either. I hang it up on the coat rack where it belongs. Do what I have to to look busy. Leaf through a few pages without really reading them.

But it's not Olga. It's my office neighbor, the eternal sports enthusiast, David. I sense that he's considering popping in to say hi, now that the door's actually open.

I remain sitting completely still. Then, luckily, he goes into his own office.

I check my inbox but there's nothing from Olga. What I *have* received, though, is the faculty's weekly newsletter in which it states that Britta's discourse analytical didactical project has been approved for funding once again. Now how is that possible? Britta is a total forage harvester when it comes to funding applications even though all she ever does is force open doors that are already open. Someone ought to write about this abysmal state of affairs. It strikes me that *I* ought to write about this abysmal state of affairs. I ought to be the one who takes on the task of unmasking her and all the others who are being overly funded because from the look of some of those theses that you see being published and those reports that are being written, well...

But it isn't your money, I say to myself. What do you care? Just stick to your own business. That makes me calm down a little.

And remember, you have your database of signs. At least *that's* real.

(No smoking)

When I come home

Annika asks me how I feel about the fact that Åsa and Lena have now been invited as well. She says it nonchalantly, in a tone of voice indicating that it's not all that important to her even though it clearly is.

That's totally fine with me, I answer. And add: It's your birthday, you're the one who should decide everything. It'll all be just the way you want it.

We're having this conversation in the kitchen because in a moment we'll be making dinner together. But then her telephone rings. She checks the display, nods to me and disappears into the living room.

Well, I guess I have no choice but to start cooking dinner by myself, then. I pour cold water into a large pot, place it on the stove and add some salt. I start looking for the pasta that the girls always like in the long cupboard as Annika continues speaking in a low voice to someone or other in the living room.

It probably has something to do with the birthday I say to myself as I chop the onions. Afterward, I pick the stems off of the tomatoes, and realize that I just have time enough to run down with the sorted garbage that is under the sink before the water starts boiling but then I notice that Annika is standing by the bedroom door. Why is she doing that?

I want to ask her who she was on the phone with and if she'll come and help me with the cooking like she promised but she just keeps standing there and that's when she sort of pushes her behind out toward me, like the animals do in the forest when they want to show off their greatest asset. The girls are playing out in the big playground that borders on our backyard. In that sense it's pretty good timing.

I go over to her, kiss her on the mouth and open the door to the bedroom. Less than a minute later her big white behind is bare and her wet crack is open.

And while I'm doing it with Annika so that the whole forest is shaking and the water out in the kitchen probably is boiling over I can't help thinking about Olga. I know it's stupid, but let it be stupid, then, because I just can't help it.

The next morning there's a message from Olga in my inbox

in which she apologizes for not turning up as we had agreed but something came up. She doesn't say what. However, what she does say is that she has concluded that she would like to do something on Kierkegaard.

"Do something on Kierkegaard"? What's wrong with the "The Great Nordic War?" Whatever happened to the idea of expanding her paper?

I'm sitting at the table with the girls eating breakfast. They're both very tired today.

Through the thin wall to the bathroom I can hear that Annika is taking a bath. We've only lived in the house for a good two months and I have reached the conclusion that we lost out on the bargain big time. As it turns out, we've bought a house made of cardboard, one of those modern gingerbread houses in which all sounds are automatically amplified.

Annika comes out with a big gray terry towel wrapped around her waist. She's wearing a bathing cap so that her hair won't get wet. She claims that washing her hair more than three times a week makes it go limp and thin. I'm not prone to disagreeing with her.

I smile at her as she closely passes me by. She smiles back. I kiss her on the neck. She goes into our bedroom and shuts the door behind her. It would seem that we're in a good phase right now.

I am just about to follow her to give her another kiss when I hear a bing sound. Another message has arrived, right on top of the other. It's Olga.

She asks whether we can meet on the twelfth. She writes that that would suit her really well. That's impossible, I begin to write, for according to my calendar the 12th falls on a Sunday and on Sundays the SOL building, the Centre for Languages and Literature building, is all locked up. But that's as far as I get because Sundays are also when the SOL building is completely deserted, which means it would just be the two of us in that great big building.

This can't possibly lead to anything good

I say to myself as I look out the window. Olga is busy locking her bike. Then she takes her bag off the luggage rack, opens it and rummages through it. She takes her time. Sweeps a strand of hair behind her ear. Takes out her cell phone. Writes something or other.

I hear two small bings behind me as my cell phone vibrates on my writing desk. Oh, that's right. We had agreed that she was to text me so that I could let her into the building. I rush out to the hallway and down the stairs, press on the square white button that makes the door swing open.

She smiles and follows me up to my office, sits down before I have asked her to in the chair that is not intended for advisory sessions like this, but I let that go for now, because there is the faint scent of a very distinct characteristic perfume lingering about her and she is wearing a red denim jacket. Under that she is wearing a dress. It's also red, which is totally fine with me. As she opens her linen bag which comes, of course, from the Strand Bookstore in New York, I suddenly catch myself wondering how it would look if one of my colleagues were to drop by the building on a Sunday like this. Olga places a notebook on my writing desk and smiles at me and I reach the conclusion that there is no actual law against supervising one's student on a Sunday. At the most it might be considered a little unusual.

She begins by admitting that she hasn't gotten started yet but that we could still discuss what she *plans* on writing. I tell her that it would have been better if she, as we had initially agreed, had sent me a few lines before the meeting, which I could have reviewed.

She nods with a serious expression on her face and we talk about what a solid research question looks like. After I have explained to her that a reassessment wouldn't be out of place since things can so easily become insipid as we have seen with regard to certain discourse analytical projects, I start talking about Søren Aabye Kierkegaard and take my time explaining the concepts to her.

She interrupts me and says that she isn't entirely sure whether she has properly understood everything, least of all the part about necessity and possibility. I tell her that it's not all that straightforward, either, but it might help if she were to consider the animal kingdom. Take the pig, for example, that runs around shitting and eating and reproducing itself without a thought in the world other than getting dirty. That, you see, is necessity, pure and simple, which can be wonderful in a way, but then there is also the notion of *possibility*, because we humans don't have to just live from one moment to the next like that at the complete mercy of our instincts and drives, we can *choose* to do something else. It is Kierkegaard in a nutshell and, which I'm sure you've already come to understand Olga, there is a whole lot of Heidegger and Sartre mixed into this, but don't forget that it was our very own beloved Kierkegaard who was the first to come up with the idea and when humans realize the responsibility that comes with choosing or choosing not to choose, that's when *anxiety* arises. And, let me tell you, anxiety is like staring down into a black abyss where you really try getting singed and burned and singed again, and the dizzying...

Oh, so you don't know what I mean by abyss? Okay, well, let's go back to the pigs then, I say, thinking to myself

that she could at least have exposed a little bit of herself to
me, now that I've been kind enough to arrange to come
in here on a Sunday on my day off. Always be cautious,
I hear myself say, when having to choose between pears
and apples, then for God's sake stay away from quinces,
and now my hand has, entirely of its own accord, inched
over to a place where the sun never touches. And as we
continue talking about Kierkegaard and choices and all the
other stuff I think it is remarkable how lively and soft she
is between her legs.

I didn't think you could tell by looking at me

but apparently you can because Annika is keeping an eye on me as I stroll around on my own through the plant nursery that resembles more of a supermarket because the living plants have been lined up on the shelves as they were detergent or Coca-cola.

It's actually possible, I realize now, to purchase a soda at the check-out because there has to be something for the kids, too. There always has to be something for the kids. That's just how it is.

I catch myself putting my fingers up to my nose, because they have a heavy scent of Olga which overpowers all the scents of the plant nursery. I had been forced to disrupt what I was busy doing with Olga because a text message from Annika beeped in the middle of it all.

"I'm on my way," she had written, "if you haven't forgotten, we promised to bring the girls along to the plant nursery."

Whereupon I got busy. As in very busy. I lent Olga my worn copy of *Either/Or* and dispatched her out the door.

Five minutes later I was standing outside, all ready and smiling, when Annika swung into the parking lot with the girls in the back seat. I saw Olga biking away somewhere in the distant background.

The shopping cart which I have picked and which doesn't in the least resemble the shopping carts you usually get at supermarkets because it is unnaturally high and shallow and has a wobbly wheel which means I have to practically push it sideways across the aisles, which is further complicated by the fact that there are garden hoses lying around everywhere.

Have you touched anything? Annika asks. She has snuck up on me without my noticing it.

She pulls my hand up to her nose and sniffs it. It smells good, she says. By the way, I've bought some lavender and hibiscus.

2

I think that seems like the best thing

I say and wipe my mouth with my napkin, Annika nods. She's wearing a yellow summer dress which I've never seen before.

We've driven to Simrishamn to take a look at Måns Byckara's party rooms, where we have sampled a version of the birthday menu which was to our great satisfaction. The wine, which was of a reasonable price range, wasn't to be scoffed at either. And that is what we tell the owner, who must be Måns, when he comes over to our table. His glasses are perched on top of his forehead and he is very sun-tanned.

Annika says that she thinks we should go for the blue room. Måns nods.

I say that I think the blue one looks more dark brown and that the amount of daylight that it gets is not exactly what one might wish for.

Måns doesn't agree with me. He sides completely with Annika. Now she is the one nodding. In fact, those two seem to agree on just about everything.

Afterward, we go down toward the water holding hands because this is our "adult weekend." The girls are with her parents. We're spending the night at Hotel Svea. It's kind of like being young again, we both agree, but I sense that we have to make an effort. Our conversations don't flow the way they used to.

Which makes me wonder, because we are both really making an effort. But is that maybe the whole problem? That we're making an effort?

I say to her that I'm not entirely sure whether Måns

is the right place after all. She doesn't answer. When the pedestrian street opens up toward the harbor square and I see seagulls and clouds and it smells of seaweed and ice cream cone wafers, I start to think of Olga.

It seems that there are others

who want to show off their attributes as well, because that is what Malin has been talking about for a good while now as we drink coffee. My breasts are natural, and they are mine, she says, and they are not to be pornofied and concealed. She says that she refuses to accept the rape culture that is pervading society at the moment.

I can see that the other two men at the coffee break table, David and Christer, are busy forming an impression of what is hiding underneath Malin's sweater and which she apparently flashes around at the swimming pool.

I understand what you mean, I say, but I don't necessarily think that your methods of action are all that good.

I take a sip of my steaming hot coffee and it is completely quiet for a moment.

What do you mean "aren't all that good"? Malin asks so defensively that Christer and David are clearly curious to see how I'm going to get out of this one, but I'm not going to get myself out of a damn thing because I don't intend to spare her from anything, least of all the truth.

Even though it's wrong as wrong can be, I say, I think it might do you some good to know that the men who click on to your website, which is, incidentally, boring as hell, and voice their sympathy, do it for one reason alone: to look at breasts, whether they be big breasts, heavy breasts, long breasts, firm breasts, or plastic breasts --even young girls' breasts have become quite popular with some I've heard it said.

And while what I'm saying may offend you, which I clearly see that it does, it doesn't really make a shit of difference because no matter how much you scold a frog for being green, the fact of the matter is that it won't stop if from being green.

I can tell that what I've just said has made some kind of an impression on her because she's sitting there with her pouty mouth half open, wanting to say something but just not sure what.

But it doesn't end there, oh no it doesn't, I continue, because we cannot rule out that some of the women who are in the habit of swimming topless in swimming pools do it just so that they can proudly show off what they normally have to hide away in their daily lives. It's just not a phenomenon that's talked about all that much, and especially not in Sweden.

It's already been a good day, a long day

in the auditorium, but I'm not done at all yet, I've actually only just begun, so I click and the next slide comes up: Hans Christian Andersen's Boulevard with traffic in both directions. Denmark's busiest street, and a little further on, by the City Hall, the rangy poet in bronze with a book in his hand. He is, by the way, also in the King's Garden *as well as* on a stamp.

I go on like that and click again, keeping, together with the asphalt and the stamp, and the other physical objects, the Hans Christian Andersen concoction brewing. That's how it is, even though the Little Mermaid is disappointing to the tourist who had expected to see something equivalent to the Eiffel Tower, the Statue of Liberty or Big Ben.

Who uses stamps anymore anyway? I ask without really knowing where I'm going with this but there's something or other in the audience that's disturbing me.

The Little Mermaid has not only resulted in a huge amount of cheap souvenirs but also musicals, ballets and movies, and in 2010 she went on a trip abroad.

Silence.

Was it really in 2010?

Yes, it was, and she was sent abroad because the architect Bjarke Ingels, by the way, in case you didn't know, he's the one who's built a skyscraper in Manhattan and in many other places in the world, sent her as far away as Shanghai where she was placed in some pavilion or other at a world exhibit at the same time that a screen had been set up on Langelinie in Denmark upon which, by way of an extremely poor internet connection, you could see the little Mermaid transmitted live from Shanghai.

I am going nowhere as I scan the audience.

There was quite an uproar about it, that is, about the fact that she was in China when she belongs on her rock in Copenhagen.

It's sort of like the Chinese buying Volvo.

No one laughs.

I suddenly notice that my armpits smell differently than they normally do and at that very moment I catch sight of the disturbing element that has slipped in during my lecture and managed to ruin everything. It's Torsten.

Torsten is standing down by the door. Torsten, a guy born with a silver spoon in his mouth. What in hell is he doing here anyway? He can't possibly be interested in Hans Christian Andersen, semiotics and high intelligence in general. There can only be one reason why he's shown up and that's to see with his own eyes the individual who has had their fingers up inside his Russian cunt.

It's all a big misunderstanding

I start my email to Olga one hour later when I'm sitting in my office, but I immediately delete it, because I'm feeling anxious. And it's not the abstract kind that we find in Kierkegaard. In a way it's a lot more concrete and it's causing a hard knot to form in the pit of my stomach. Things don't get better when, right before going home, I receive a text message from Britta saying she has a matter she would like to discuss with me at a convenient time. Which isn't good because she doesn't mention anything about what the matter pertains to. Is there a sexual harassment case in store for me? Is that where we're at now? The world won't take kindly to such a situation. And Annika definitely won't, either.

(Fibrillator)

We are watching something on television

the same evening. Annika is sitting on the couch, her legs tucked under her in the sofa and we've just started a new season of *Orange Is the New Black* on Netflix. I don't think it's quite on the same level as the previous seasons because not a damn thing happens and what's not happening is happening too damn slowly.

I'm not really into this, I say to Annika as the prisoners dressed in orange jumpsuits run through a hole in the fence and bathe in a nearby lake to the soundtrack of sweet music.

But Annika doesn't agree. Far from it. She says I have to be more open to the new ideas that the series has to offer and she starts explaining to me that what we are witnessing is a new kind of literature in moving pictures. Okay, I answer, I guess she knows what she's talking about because she has defended a thesis in literary sciences on how working class Swedish literature was received by the British Isles in the 1930's. I've only skimmed through the thesis, but I've been told that it is chock-full of the kind of knowledge that is beneficial for all mankind.

She's also written several articles dealing with the fact that beech trees and oak trees often appear in Danish poetry, while in Swedish and Finnish poetry the trees are often coniferous which says a great deal about the different forms of plant life in each country.

I realize that Annika is looking at me instead of following the drama on the screen, and that takes a lot. I quickly give her a smile, but am apparently too slow. She hits the pause button and asks me how I'm doing. You've seemed a little quiet lately, she says.

I answer that I've had a few setbacks at work but that it looks like things are straightening out. The picture on the pause screen shows one of the inmates sweeping the prison yard as the others are either playing basketball or smoking. They are back behind the high prison fence and everything's back to normal.

Britta seems stressed and a little stiff.

but on the other hand she always does, so it doesn't necessarily mean anything. So far she's told me how grateful she is to have received her huge grant money and I've told her that I'm happy for her. I've also said that she fully deserves it.

But I still don't understand what this meeting is all about.

She has asked me how I am faring at work and whether I like the areas of responsibility that have been assigned to me. I've answered that all things considered I have nothing to complain about, which corresponds to the truth.

Then there's the issue of the spring party, she says dryly, as though this is something that suddenly just entered her mind and yet perhaps not so suddenly. I understand that you are on the party committee? And that is why, she continues, I would like to know why you haven't attended the meetings you've been summoned to.

She looks straight at me and I look straight back at her. Now is the time for me to come up with an answer, I know that, but I just don't have one. At least not one that is all that useful. It could be a question of emails that due to my otherwise excellent-functioning system may have fallen between the cracks. Emails are flowing in all directions, so I go by a principle that says one email is the equivalent of no emails. Not unless the sender goes out of his or her way to send another email can I be sure that they have something important to communicate to me. But that probably doesn't explain everything- Malin Gujord is in charge of the committee and I can't stand Malin Gujord.

I tell Britta that it is, of course, due to a mistake on my part and that it won't happen again and that I'll rectify it.

Yes, she says, because there is no need to cause a conflict that won't be to anyone's benefit in the end.

Is that all? I ask, almost feeling a sense of relief. Yes, that's all.

Well, thank you then, I say and leave.

3

The most powerful sign in my sign collection

can make me cry. I took a picture of it at Wien Sudbahnhoff when I was down there on a prolonged weekend trip with Annika. Without the kids. It was placed on the track on which the overcrowded trains that transported Syrian refugees pulled in.

Information was given in several languages besides German and English that the Austrian authorities wore yellow vests and that it was important to have your passport ready. Other imminent procedures were mentioned. The list concluded with a sentence that all at once cut away everything but this one fact, cut to the very heart of the matter and left only one thing: *You are safe.*

That's exactly how I see my own situation right now. I've been down a slippery slope where I've found myself in some disaster area and where my personal life, my career, just about everything, have been at stake, but I'm beginning to feel that I'm finally safe now. I haven't heard from Olga for weeks and I haven't seen a trace of Torsten.

It feels good and I'm certain that everything has finally settled down. And why shouldn't it? Things don't always have to develop into the worst possible scenarios.

I click on Spotify at the bottom of the screen and activate a playlist of Love Shop, which I made a few days ago. It's the kind of music that doesn't pretend to be something that it isn't. I've considered whether I should give Annika a pair of concert tickets to see them as a birthday present. One for me and one for her. Though she's said that they probably aren't really her cup of tea, I'm convinced that that'll change once we hear them together live. She just needs to give them a chance.

Annika isn't at home. She sent me a message an hour ago. She was very sorry but she had to work late today. She is responsible for, along with another colleague, planning the upcoming outing. I had actually forgotten that she was going on one of those trips. But she is apparently.

I'll go to the parents' meeting at Lark's school, I write back. I can't stand parents' meetings but it's just one of those things you have to accept.

As the rhythms to Love shop's "En nat bliver det sommer" begin, I shift my focus back to my signs, skim through my archives. I have classified them according to the country from which they derive, what they indicate, their physical design and the history which they contain. My father-in-law has said that I'm a stamp collector, only I collect signs instead. I have to agree with him. *Ich bin ein stamp collector.*

Welcome

We have prepared for supporting you during your stay
and as you continue your journey

Members of the Austrian Federal Railways (OBB)
Caritas the Vienna paramedics and the police are
here at the railway station to meet you

You can recognise all members of the assistance team
by their special clothing If you have any questions
please do not hesitate to ask them

Many Viennese are supporting us as we distribute
food and water to you Interpreters (translators) are
available Any medical assistance you may need can
be provided on site

We are doing our very best to organise assistance

You are safe

The City of Vienna

Hedenhös School is now certifiably gender sanitized

the school principal informed us as though a delousing of sorts had taken place. I drink red wine and listen to Love Shop to help me get through the parents' meeting.

Male plugs and female plugs. They don't buy that in Sweden. Though I definitely believe that we humans contain many different personalities within us, I'm not exactly keen on the idea that our gender exists only in our minds. The world becomes just a bit too tame then as far as I'm concerned.

I can hear the door down there now. Annika's coming. It's also 8:30 pm now but perhaps we can still manage to watch an episode of *Orange is the New Black* before we go to bed. I also wouldn't mind having another glass of red wine and hearing her opinion on male plugs and female plugs.

It's summer, it's sunny, the sun is shining and it's Sunday

I'm sitting at the garden table with the day's edition of the Danish newspaper Politiken and a cup of coffee in front of me. Annika is puttering about in the garden. It has to look nice, our garden, because she's decided that she would rather celebrate her birthday here at home. It's much cozier in one's own private surroundings. You don't really intend to have the party in our little yard, do you? I asked. Yes, indeed, she did. You were the one who wasn't crazy about Måns, she answered.

In the newspaper there's a wonderful, double-page article about me and my research. I took the train to Copenhagen in order to get a copy this morning. Annika and the kids didn't want to join me but that's up to them. I'm considering framing the picture and hanging it up in my office.

There are a few minor mistakes in the article, but never mind about that. The picture, on the other hand, is good. The photographer wanted me to stand in front of the bookcase in the living room. At first I said that I thought that was a cheesy idea. Is that so it'll look like I read a lot of books? I asked. But the interview is about your demographic mapping of people's reading habits, he said, and luckily that made me change my mind. The books on the bookshelves of Nørrebro aren't the same as the ones on the bookshelves of Østerbro and if we take a quick look at what books I myself have…

At this point Annika waves at me and I wave back. I drink a little coffee. It's turned cold. She is holding her hand up to her forehead to shield her eyes from the sun.

Her eyes are gray, even though we've agreed on referring to them as green. She is completely different from Olga. True, she has bigger breasts, but to be completely honest, they're a little heavy and on the matronly side. She hasn't said anything about why she got home so late last night and I haven't wanted to ask. I'm sure there was a perfectly good reason for it and anyway, we shouldn't have to monitor one another in that way. Not in a healthy relationship.

Annika starts digging once again with her light spade. She's on her knees and her behind is sticking up a lot. Isn't she also starting to get a little pear-shaped? That's what's happened to all her prim, geranium friends. Soon they'll all be coming for the birthday and filling the garden with pears where we otherwise only have quinces.

It's incredible how far your thoughts can wander if you let them. Where am I getting all these sudden whims from? I love Annika. She has a nice ass and heavy breasts. What kind of a person have I become? It's the thing with Olga that's still alive within me. Perhaps it would help if I came clean and told Annika about my little affair? Just to get it out of my system.

On the other hand, that wouldn't really do anyone any good. We've lived together now for almost twelve years. When it comes to infidelity, the record was set straight from the very start: it's totally out of the question. All right, so there may have been a few slip-ups on my part, but that was just back when we got started, before we had the girls, so it doesn't really count, and as far as my past life goes before I met Annika, well, we can, for good reasons, completely disregard that part of my life altogether.

I am standing in the assembly hall by the staircase leading to the basement

waiting for Malin. The last two folding tables have to be carried up. The party isn't until next Friday but Malin thinks it's important that we get a quick overview of the tables and chairs we have at our disposal. They first have to be piled up in the Faculty Club. I've wondered whether it would be possible to borrow the tables and matching chairs for Annika's birthday. That would make things somewhat cheaper. Then all I'd need is to find a party tent.

It's pouring outside. Outside of the Joint Faculties of Humanities and Theology building, also known as the LUX building, students and employees can be seen running around. They've pretty much deserved that, because over there, just on the other side of Professor Square where theology and philosophy are located, they've gotten all the latest hardware installed that one could ever dream of in the classrooms. Here at the SOL building we have to make do with last year's winter trend in teaching materials.

Why isn't Malin coming? Does she think we're through here? For most of the afternoon she's been ordering everyone and everything around. Walking around with her long list and making check marks and taking down notes so that we don't forget anything. It's completely unbearable.

I suddenly start: Olga! She must just have stepped through the main entrance door. She is standing in the middle of the auditorium wearing a long raincoat. Her hair has grown longer since I last saw her. Perhaps she's just changed her hairdo. She catches sight of me. She hesitates for a moment, and then it's as though she makes a decision. She walks straight toward me.

She says hello and before I get the chance to say anything she apologizes for not having contacted me. It's because my mother's been sick, she says, but I'm not entirely convinced. For most of my adult life I've worked with young people and I know that youth can be carefree and unpredictable and that its dealings with truth are oftentimes careless. She asks whether she has wasted her chance of working with me and I say that it would take a lot more than that.

Why are you standing here? she then asks. I look for Malin, where the hell can she be? I say that I was actually supposed to fetch some tables for the staff party in the basement but that I quite frankly don't know where my colleague has disappeared to and that I'm not exactly equipped with four hands.

No sooner have I said those words than I come to realize what door I have unintentionally opened. And sure enough, Olga says, let me help you!

I smile and remind myself that I'm a big boy who can easily decline an offer.

STILLA RUM

Alla oavsett trosuppfattning ar varmt valkomna

Rummet ar avsett for enskild eftertanke inte for organiserad verksamhet for storre eller mindre grupper

Oppet under SOL s ordinarie oppettider

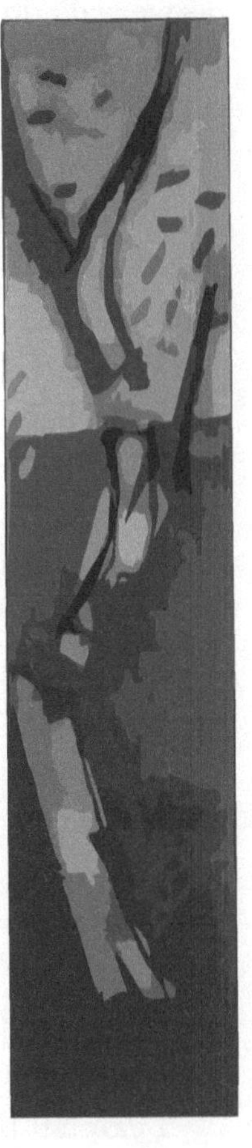

(Quiet Room: Everyone regardless of their religious faith is welcome. The room is intended for individual meditation and not for group activities of any kind. Open during SOL's normal opening hours).

I notice a small sizzling sensation in the lower part of my body

as we walk down the linoleum staircase. Olga's scalp, she is three steps ahead of me on the stairs, reveals a considerably lighter shade at the hair roots. It looks like a home hair dying job, the kind that's typically done at the kitchen counter. That, together with the jeans she's wearing and her eager feet laced in their white sneakers, give a childish impression.

Where is it? she asks when we get down to the basement and the light turns on automatically. We look down the wide corridor of red bricks with heavy metal doors on either side.

All the way at the bottom, I say. Okay, she says. Should we walk down there? I ask. All right, she says in a voice that sounds like we were embarking on an unknown trip to Africa.

She stops at a wall painting which some students made several years ago. The theme is classical works from the history of literature. I've never understood why they made it down here where it's completely hidden away and no one ever sees it. I tell her that. And then I continue: And here we have Don Quixote's windmills, Dante's inferno, and the Cyclops from the Odyssey.

I can tell that she isn't listening and before I'm finished she starts to walk on. She's like a child who is easily distracted. I have no problem with that.

What's this? she asks as we pass a door that is dark blue and not gray like the others. "Quiet Room" it says on the sign by the door which could have been hung a bit straighter. I explain that it's a prayer room which SOL set up a few years ago for the Muslims who are employed there. They have to pray a certain amount of times a day. Olga asks whether she can have a look at the "Quiet Room." Yes, of course you can. I can't see why not.

There is a small, quick "switch" sound as I place my digital card against the black button on the door handle.

The door is surprisingly heavy because the rooms down here were originally built as air-raid shelters of sorts. Probably from way back when the Soviet Union, which is, in fact, where Olga comes from, posed the greatest threat.

She walks in first. The lights are dim because the illuminators that run along the middle of the walls on each side are placed behind a wooden panel. There is a low green couch at the end wall with a small mirror above it. On the floor lies a piece of paper with an arrow pointing toward the direction of Mecca.

Olga stands with her back toward me as she looks around, she is so incredibly young and curious. I can see her reflection in the mirror. She doesn't have the faintest clue what's awaiting her as I shut the big shelter door behind us. It doesn't seem as though she's registered it. We are truly deep in the jungle now.

She says, mostly to herself, that it's a fine gesture on behalf of the university to have made this room available for that purpose.

I agree with her. And as I do I slip my hand underneath her long rain coat and cautiously squeeze one of her breasts. It doesn't fill more than a handful.

She doesn't react. She stands with her arms at her sides and lets me do whatever I want with her small breast.

There's something trance-like about the situation. I also kiss her on the back of her neck. She smells the same way she did the first time I touched her in my office. Even though she's standing still I sense that she's full of life. Her heart is pounding wildly under my hands which have both made their way underneath her raincoat. She's gotten this distant look in her eyes as though she's suddenly grown tired. I start unbuttoning her jeans. Her stomach, her flat stomach, is now visible, her white Russian skin. Light blue underpants with a tiny ribbon on the edge.

Suddenly she takes over, as though I'm too slow. Placing two fingers on each side, she pulls down her underwear and pants in one long movement, just like that, because that's how they are, young people, always ready to perform the sex act. In their world it's an uncomplicated affair, so it's always just a matter of striking whenever the possibility arises.

As I penetrate her I catch myself thinking that there certainly is such a thing as a male plug and a female plug, in case anyone's in doubt. And aside from that, we'd better just hope there aren't too many Russian diseases in there.

I knew she was young, but still:

Born in '94. I wouldn't have guessed that. She hadn't even come out of her mother's womb yet when I met Annika.

I've been snooping around on Olga's Facebook page for a good hour now. Why shouldn't I? I can see she's had a few little gigs as a fashion model in St. Petersburg and done a little jazz ballet. In one of her latest posts she writes that she's become infatuated with Søren Kierkegaard and Copenhagen. I convince myself that that's just to cover up something else. But if she wants to learn more about Denmark, I'd be happy to be the one to help her on her way.

In one of her photo albums from last summer most of the pictures are of her and Torsten. She's practically clinging to him. She's clinging to him aboard a sailboat that probably belongs to his father. She's clinging to him at a champagne bar and even as he attempts to play beach volleyball with the guys. She still clings to him, because Torsten is a little conceited twerp.

4

Hi, says Olga

as though it were the most natural thing in the world. Hi! I answer in a subdued voice.

David's door is open and I know that the eternal handball player is sitting in there listening with all his might. I think he's noticed that she's stopped by a few times earlier. Twice just in this past week.

I can't talk right now, I say in a somewhat louder voice hoping that David will hear it. I haven't had a chance to read your proposal draft of a problem formulation...

She smiles complicitly, pops into my office and shuts the door behind her. She is dazzlingly beautiful. She most certainly is. Her superb, brilliant cheekbones, her dark hair, not to mention her long legs. I especially appreciate those. All right, so maybe she radiates a certain hardness and firmness but don't we find that in all Russians?

We can't meet here, I say. What about the place where we fetched the table? she asks. That is, of course, a possibility, I say. I nod. She disappears, her eyes shining.

I calmly turn toward the computer screen and save the document I've been working on. A series of lectures for the People's University and the Nordic Association that will pinpoint, in an entertaining way, what basic national elements we have in Denmark. So far I've written about our defeat to the Prussians in 1864, the folk high school movement, and allotment gardens. I'll soon start on Danish design. Arne Jakobsen and all the rest. I think it's going to be really good.

I get up from my chair and walk out into the hallway but take a moment to pop in and say hi to David. We exchange a few trivialities about handball. He tells me that he's considering studying to become a referee. There's a course coming up in September. On second thought, it's probably in October, but he's convinced that it's just the thing for him.

Well, good luck with it, then, and thanks for the chat, I say and start heading toward the basement. I walk as though I were out to get a cup of coffee in the staff room. I might also be on my way to a meeting. You can't tell. I realize that everything I do right now is so rehearsed that that in itself is liable to draw attention.

That's because I'm having an affair. That's how it is. You're having an affair.

It is, of course, terrible, but also, how can one put it, wonderfully life-affirming and it gives me an unfamiliar sense of excitement. It's as though I've returned to the summer of my youth. I didn't know I had it in me. But apparently I do.

You seem to have a thing with signs, Olga says.

Yes, I have a thing with signs, I answer. We are sitting furthest out on the bathing jetty in Habo Ljung. It goes way out because the water is very shallow here. Denmark is just across on the other side of Øresund. I can see a few chimneys and some tall buildings. Perhaps the national hospital is among them. Both my daughters were born there when we were still living in Copenhagen.

Where did you find this one? Olga asks, indicating the ugliest sign in my collection. expressing something that resembles genuine interest.

I explain that back when I was a university student I would bike every day along Hans Christian Andersen's Boulevard, cross the bridge to Amager and turn right by the SAS hotel and there, a ways in on some land, right before reaching KUA, stood an old house.

KUA? Olga asks. Yes, it's short for Copenhagen University Amager.

She is wearing a yellow linen shirt with no bra underneath. She knows how her breasts affect me. We know each other better now and she lets me see whatever I want.

I can see she's waiting for me to continue and so that's what I do.

It was a beautiful house built with the best materials that was made into a two-story dorm. I think all in all eight students resided there, I say. But that's actually beside the point. On the garden gate, which was made of wrought iron, a sign had been put up which said, *This gate is to be kept closed at all times.*

She has goose bumps on her lower legs. It isn't quite summer yet even though there are some Germans who've already arrived at the campsite in back of us.

She wants to know what it was I thought was so bad about that sign. Well, you see, I explain, the young people who resided there and who passed through this beautiful house, were confronted with that message day in and day out, this utterly negative reminder, both when they returned home and when they were on their way out into the world.

But if they had taken the sign literally, she said thoughtfully, then they would never have gone anywhere, would they? Neither out nor in. No, that's a good point, I say.

(Recently introduced gender neutral pronoun that can be used instead of masculine "han" and feminine "hun.")

We have dined at the Grand Hotel

with Annika's parents and are standing in the lobby where my mother-in-law is being handed her big black coat. The food was outstanding, four dishes with the perfect wines to go with them. It was my father-in-law's treat. He wanted to celebrate the fact that his office pension had come in.

It was very generous of him, of course. The bill amounted to almost 2300 for four people, but I still can't help but feel a little disappointed. When something good happens, there is typically a trickle-down effect, but when you think about the size of that good thing he's received, about two million I think it was, one could have expected a little bit more.

I have suggested to Annika that she might gingerly ask him whether it would be possible to receive a small contribution to the carport we are considering having built. We could, at first, just call it a loan, I say. She's very reluctant. I don't see why you can't, I say to her. We'll be getting that money at some point anyway, and you don't have any siblings. So that can't be the problem.

She's agreed to think about it.

As we are standing on the stone staircase outside the restaurant and are exchanging our good-byes, my mood sinks even further, because that's when I catch sight of Olga and she isn't alone. She is walking with Torsten and they are talking complicitly, almost eagerly, with one another. My impression is that they are coming from the train station. In other words, they've been riding a train together, and they shouldn't do that.

That shouldn't be a problem

I answer, perhaps a little abruptly. It's Olga. She's sent me a message. She'd like to meet. As soon as possible. She has something important she wants to discuss with me.

I'm actually busy preparing my lecture for the Nordic Association. "You Can't Get Lost in Denmark" is the heading of the powerpoint I'm working on. I've been searching for a map of Denmark that depicts our small country with all the water surrounding it. We are a seafaring nation, I write, but immediately cross it out again because it's really important not to get caught up in unnecessary details and go off on too many tangents.

So: You can't get lost in Denmark. 1) It is never more than just 45 km to the coast and 2) We no longer have any big forests which you can hide in. No matter where you are situated, you will, sooner or later, run into a group of schoolchildren with their lunch bags or a dog walker who is out, well, walking his dog. And speaking of animals: looking for wildlife? Well, you can forget all about it. We have neither bears nor whales. Several years ago an elk swam across to Denmark from Sweden. That's all. Sparrows, squirrels and porcupines are about all we have to offer.

I wonder what animal Olga would be if she were an animal?

There is something or other the matter with her

I think as I open the big blue door. And I can see that I'm right as she walks in and turns toward me.

She seems sad. That's what she seems. But I can't really see how she could be because just a few days ago I saw her skipping down the street with Torsten.

How are you? I ask. She shakes her head and sits down on the sofa. She says that her mother is very sick. I ask her whether she's taken the train lately. That's something I'd really like to know. She looks at me with a disoriented expression. She says she doesn't really understand what I mean. I say that I saw her the other day by the train station. You were together with Torsten, if I'm not mistaken. She smiles and wipes away a tear. She says it was just because they are both on the committee for the Malmø Festival, something they've been on for a long time now and she doesn't feel that she can just abandon it now when there are only two months left before the festival. The others are counting on her, she says. I understand that in a way, I say, but it's also important to know where you belong and that you're capable of making a decision. Decisions are important.

She agrees with me on that. She also says that that festival actually isn't important at all. It's so commercial anyway. Now it's my turn to agree with her. I've been there myself a few times with Annika and the children. It's as though the festival doesn't know which leg to stand on. There's a trapeze castle for the kids, music for the younger crowd at Stortorget, and sample tasting for the older crowd.

But it doesn't seem to have a real profile of its own. You have to really search high and low for that. Olga smiles and says that, at any rate, she plans on leaving it when it's all over and done with in August and so she might as well do it now. I tell her that she shouldn't do it for my sake, but I would understand if she chooses to drop it.

I'm standing right in front of her. She looks up at me quizzically. I gather her long black hair at the back of her neck. Even pull it a little. She reciprocates my kiss when I lean down and let my lips touch hers, but at the same time also get the feeling that she isn't altogether there, that she doesn't really feel like it. But we might as well do it now that we're here anyway. That's probably how she's thinking too. At any rate, she allows herself to fall back in the sofa as I carefully push her backwards and she even lifts her behind so that I can remove her underwear.

The sight of her naked lower body is utterly fantastic and even though at the beginning she stares into the wall with her face turned away, it's not as though she doesn't let my fingers wander wherever they want to and I also succeed fairly quickly in getting everything to move down there.

There was something wrong
with that moment

in the basement, I know that. I'm sitting in the metro under Nørreport station on my way to give the first lecture in the series about Denmark but I'm struggling to collect my thoughts. What was it Olga had said without really saying it?

When we were through with what we had come for she reclined into the sofa with her legs tucked under her and without putting her clothes back on. I thought that was strange. She had said that her mother's illness was serious-lung cancer. She had also cried. I said to her that I was very sorry to hear that. She had hoped, she said, to at least get the chance to travel back home and see her before it was too late but that she didn't have the money for it.

The doors slide open. Amagerbro Station. There's a dog sitting in the passageway with its tongue hanging out of its mouth as it stares at me. I won't be getting off until Frederiksberg Station. Is it really allowed to take your dog with you on the metro? The owner is an older man in a jogging suit and wearing a headband. They've probably been out running together on Amager Fælled or Femøren.

I ignore the dog and glance through my notes. It would be good if I could manage to memorize them. It would give that extra boost. Sweden is a modern industrial society whereas Denmark is more of a, shall we say, domicile for nostalgia and traditions. I glance at my notes: Gammel Dansk, *Matador*, Tivoli, *Father of Four in the Snow.* I see that I've also written that Denmark is a pronounced agricultural country, which I'm not entirely sure is true, but according to Statistics Denmark, there are more pigs than people in Denmark.

Yes, there are undoubtedly plenty of swine here and come to think of it, aren't you a bit of an old pig yourself? I mean, what kind of a situation are you beginning to find yourself in without wanting to admit it because it's suddenly starting to get complicated? Or, unaffordable, rather? What was it Olga was trying to say to you? Isn't there a fair chance that she actually expects you to pay for her trip to Russia and back? Was that it? Is that what it's come to, a kind of blackmail? She is clearly out to get your money. Your hard-earned savings.

I would have preferred not to have to have this conversation

says Britta as she looks directly at me. That certainly goes for me too, I think.

It is Malin. The party is in two days and she has let it leak out that she feels a little abandoned. She's told Britta that she hasn't been getting the support she might have expected.. For example, she had to ask the custodian to help her get the last tables from the basement and that is just too much. And Britta agrees with her.

I say that I would be the first one to regret that. I don't really feel that I can say that it won't happen again. That one's already been used.

But what is going to happen in the future? Britta asks fixing her gaze on me behind her big glasses suggesting that she has great confidence in Malin, whereas the extent to which I can contribute anything is a different story.

Yes, what will happen in the future? I begin but then get stuck.

She is waiting but I really don't know what to say because I know that I've already lost the battle. There was never really any chance for me to begin with. I know that those two women are close friends and that they sometimes go to the Ystad Saltwater Pool together where they, in the company of other females, sink their auntie-pear-shaped bodies into a great variety of whirlpools and jacuzzis. Something which I, of course, could never partake in.

I pull myself together and say that I'll just have to put my back into it in this final phase.

Thank you for coming, Britta says and suggests that I sign up for the clean-up committee.

You're welcome, I say and get to my feet.

She gives me a cool look, as though I'm of utter insignificance as I walk over to the door.

What is this all about?

A new email from Olga. She writes that she's very unhappy and is therefore unable to continue her work on the assignment. She plans to make her final decision after the summer break, but right now that's how things look. She concludes with a bunch of emojis. There are even some that I can't decipher. 

I am therefore not entirely sure as to what it is she's trying to tell me, so I just stare blankly at the computer screen.

When I have sat like that for a considerable period of time the lights suddenly go out because when you sit still without moving, the hidden sensors begin to register you as an object in the room which makes the lights go out.

Who is Henrik?

I ask. The display screen on Annika's cellphone lying next to the sink has started to light up because she's received a message. It's from someone named Henrik and I can't help but read it as I stand here brushing my teeth. It says: Should we say 7 pm, then?

Annika is sitting behind me and taking a pee. She dries herself and flushes the toilet. She positions herself next to me and looks at her reflection in the mirror. Adjusts her hair.

Henrik is a colleague, she says, and he is also coming tonight, if you really want to know.

I do.

Annika dabs her wrists with perfume and rubs them just behind her ears.

Okay, I say and rinse my mouth. Where will you be eating?

Probably at Glorya's, she answers a little too quickly.

But isn't that primarily a sports bar?

Maybe it is.

She walks out of the bathroom and into the bedroom. I follow behind her.

How many do you think you'll be?

She shrugs her shoulders.

I can come join you later if you want?

She opens her wardrobe, assessing what it has to offer. Brushes her hand across the clothes hanging in there.

You don't need to do that.

No, but I could.

I'd like to get home at a reasonable hour, she answers.

This is so typical. I'm the one who is going to a summer party at work but I'm beginning to see a pattern here: because I'm going out tonight, she insists on doing something as well.

That means that the kids will be babysat by her parents at their place again. In my opinion she could stay at home and cozy up with the kids on a Friday evening but that's apparently completely out of the question. Is that really how she's become?

Is there anything wrong? she asks.

No, why do you ask?

I can see that the SOL choir is getting ready to go on stage

because we've already been through the obligatory quiz session and Britta has made her little summer-is-soon-approaching speech, so now it is time for choir singing. Because in Sweden we all appreciate Bellman and Taube, but I'm afraid it'll have to be without me. I need to step out and get some fresh air because I've had my share of both the red and the white. I'm the one who's been responsible for distributing the wine tickets, here you go, two for each and then a few bonus coupons for myself for doing such a good job.

But it doesn't help. Everything is still spinning around as I stand outside in front of the pond with a view of the University Library. The ducks walking by the water's edge are spinning, the bikes in the bicycle stands are spinning and even the clouds in the sky, well, they are spinning, too.

It's still incredible if you think about it. The library contains all the Scandinavian books that have ever been published up until 1950. And when I say all I mean all, and at the thought of all those wonderful books that are in that large building, it's actually as though a certain sense of tranquility comes over me and my surroundings. So just chill out! Why does everything have to be so depressing? A long summer with Annika and the girls is stretching out in front of you. Bulgaria. All inclusive. It's going to be great.

My cellphone vibrates in my pocket. I fish it out. It's Olga. She asks whether we can meet up. It's urgent, as she puts it. I'm about to write that that is unfortunately impossible because right now we're having, which she knows perfectly well, our annual summer party. Before I manage to press the send button, it dawns on me that the wheel, of course, spins the other way around, because her beautiful head is just popping up tonight when she knows I am attending the party. It's as sweet as anything can be and so instead I answer that she should come by and we'll figure something out. Meet me at the back entrance. Be a little discreet.

By the time I go back inside and get another glass of red wine a new message has arrived from Olga: Do you really mean that? I'm actually very close by. You bet! Because, again, why does life have to be so depressing? Take for example Malin, sitting at one of the long tables which she herself has struggled to carry up though the custodian helped her, looking like someone who's just sucked on a lemon. I lift my glass to her in an excessive gesture of good will but she just looks away. Then I empty the glass, down all the red wine, and up your ass, Malin. Thus rejuvenated, I go out to meet Olga. The party is just getting started.

5

I have a splitting headache,

Annika is lying next to me in the bed. Halfway entangled in the duvet wearing a yellow top that doesn't leave much to the imagination. Her one breast seems to sort of flatten itself against her body because her arm is lying across it. The other is lying pressed down against the bed. It's not a pretty sight. I wonder what time she got home last night?

There is the stench of stale alcohol in the bedroom. I hear the birds outside. Annika must have opened the window sometime during the night. What time did I actually get home? I can't remember. There's something about last night which I simply can't remember.

I sit halfway up in the bed. My head hurts. I pull on a t-shirt and leave the bedroom. I check in on the girls. They're lying each in their own wooden bed, each in their own room. I draw the curtain properly in Lark's room before putting up the coffee. Take out a can of Treo in the kitchen cabinet and plop two in a glass of cold water. Wait until the tablets have dissolved and knock back the sizzling water. The sense of unreality will probably disappear in a moment, I think. But it doesn't.

I'm taken aback when I catch sight of my pants in the hallway. They're lying open across my shoes as had I *jumped* right out of them.

The light is on in the guest bathroom, the door is standing ajar. I take a look in there. The rest of my clothes are lying in a pile next to the toilet. My watch is lying under the sink. What is this? It's all very disconcerting. Things must really have gotten out of hand last night. Everything is so muddled in my mind. I took Olga with me down to the basement, that much I remember. It was important to get her down there.

I rush to collect all my clothes and put them in the laundry bin in the bathroom on the second floor. Go back to the kitchen and pour a cup of black coffee from the coffee carafe and take it with me out into the yard.

I sit down in one of the lawn chairs that Annika's parents gave us some time ago and wait for the pills to take effect.

It's amazing the amount of small fruits growing there on the two quince trees. With time they'll definitely provide excellent shade. If, for example, we want to eat dinner out here.

I try to get myself to relax, to settle down, but there's something or other that's terribly wrong, a quiet sort of panic that won't go away.

Through the window in the scullery I can see Annika. She is looking at me. I wave at her. Her face disappears. A few moments later she comes out from the house.

Good-morning, I say. She doesn't answer right away. I can see that she's carrying the shirt I had on last night in her hand. What's this all about? she asks, holding it up before me.

There is a stain down the front side covering both sides of the buttons. It's not just a smudge, but a stain. There's no denying what it is. Blood. I take a sip of the coffee that has an intensely bitter taste to it and say that I had a nosebleed.

I don't know what compels me to say that because I know it's not true. The images that have probably been trying to make their way to the surface ever since I woke up are now beginning to take shape. Annika turns around and goes into the house. I watch her as she leaves. I don't know whether she believes me, but that's the least of my problems right now. The blood on the shirt isn't mine, of that I'm certain. This isn't about me. It's about Olga.

When a little while later I'm standing under the cold shower,

letting the water pour down over me, images from the previous evening start to flash before me. Olga at my office. Olga on my writing desk. Her mouth gets so big when she puts on lipstick. She really shouldn't wear it.

I didn't want her to sit on my writing desk, I suddenly recall, and I said so to her, too. You better get down from there. Before I knew it, she had taken my wine glass out of my hand and was taking a sip from it. I didn't want that, either. It was enough already, it had gone too far.

Her hair. It was rather dishevelled.

What was it with her? I could hear the music from the staff party far in the distance. What if someone were to come by? I thought. What if Handball David or one of the others has to pick something up from their office? What time was it, even? And how long had we been there? I know that at some point we left the office together, Olga and I. Because we were on our way to the basement, of course.

I tip over the shampoo bottle. The thick liquid runs straight into the drain. Annika won't be pleased, because it's the only shampoo that does something for her hair, that can give it some volume. I'm not even really allowed to use it.

Olga. I should never have asked her to come to the party. Of course I shouldn't have. She had dirty hands. Dirt under her fingernails. Why is that? I asked. As we were walking down to the basement she told me that she had just been visiting a girlfriend at her allotment garden. She had helped her with the weeding and they had planted a few seeds they had found in the Botanical Gardens. It was obvious that "found" really meant "stolen" and that what they had really been doing most of the day was boozing. She was drunk, just like I was.

She told me that it had been her girlfriend who had suggested that she approach me and tell it to me straight. Tell me what straight? I asked as I opened the door to the Quiet Room. I'd actually like to know that.

We should never have gone down into that damn basement.

She was naked, right?

No, she wasn't entirely naked. Only the upper part of her body was bare. She sat in the sofa, her hands folded in front of her. That's how it was. Okay, then, and what else? What happened then?

You asked her to remove them, her hands, right? You hadn't gone down there just for nothing. Try to think. She went along with it, or what? She may have, but I don't know. Who else would know, then? You're the one who knows best what happened. You're the one who woke up with blood stains on your clothes.

The water is turning cold now. I ought to turn it off and step out of the shower stall, reach out for the towel, go into the bedroom and dress and go down to the kitchen to my family but I remain standing under the cold running water because all I wanted was for the Russian to shut her damn trap. Nothing more than that.

Did she say anything about Annika? Was that it? No, I don't think so. What did she say about Annika? Had she discovered your sore point? Is that what made you finally snap?

The vibes weren't good between us so we couldn't have done it. Maybe we just went our separate ways. What else could we have done? Because nothing happened, right?

Or did it? At some point you grabbed hold of her delicate white shoulders a little too gruffly. Did you start to shake her? Was that what it was? Was it? Making her small breasts bop up and down?

And why did you do it?

I don't know if I did.

No, maybe you don't and we're not even finished yet. Is there more? Is there? Yes, because she wouldn't keep her mouth shut so you pushed her from the sofa onto the floor. Pushed?

No, hurled, rather. And this is where the blood comes into the picture. Because there was blood, we know that for a fact, and if you left her like that, then she was lying there alone in the basement, gasping for breath, her eyes rolling. And she may still be lying there.

Water is dripping from my hair to the floor

because I haven't dried it properly. I pull a pair of clean jeans out of the closet and put them on. They're stiff and my legs are white from all the cold water that's been splashed on them.

We were both highly intoxicated, no doubt about that, and so it's not really possible to remember in detail what actually happened. But the thought that I might have injured her is absurd. Most likely there is a perfectly good explanation for the blood stain on my shirt. Of course there is, but in order to put an end to that minor concern that's now arisen, I decide to stop by the SOL building.

I go out to the kitchen where Annika is busy packing a big lunch bag which I don't understand because it's Saturday. I say to her that I've been thinking about the speech I want to give on her birthday and that a lot of ideas came to me last night. I'm happy to hear that, she says. Yes, and that's why I think it might be a good idea if I spent a few hours at the institute and wrote everything down while it's all still fresh in my memory.

She looks at me, her head slightly cocked. I also have something I need photocopied for Monday, I continue, and it would be kind of nice to have that out of the way.

She smiles sheepishly and says that that's all very well and nice but it'll probably have to wait until tomorrow because I've promised to take the kids to The Blue Planet. I'd totally forgotten about that. And then I also remember that the reason why it came up was because Annika is going hiking in Genarp. Hence the lunch bag. She's going with Åsa and Lena and they're going to go fitness walking for several hours where they'll take breaks and drink tea.

Fitness walking!

I also expect some of my colleagues to join us Annika says as she places the butter in the refrigerator. When they heard about the excursion a couple of them decided to come with us.

Who are they? I ask as I smile to my girls who are on their way down the stairs. No one you know, she answers, struggling with the lid for the butter, but I think you guys should just start getting ready so you can get going.

In an aquarium there is a huge fish

that practically remains still in the water like a big lump of meat. The only thing moving on it is its lips. It's a wrasse, I am told in three different languages when I press on a yellow button. It lives off of molluscs and aquatic insects which it sucks in between its lips. Even certain starfish like the toxic crown-of-thorns sometimes lands in there. It has a somewhat calming effect, but I can't help wondering what its purpose is, the wrasse. Why do animals like that exist in the world? In another combined aquarium and terrarium some very strange-looking crustaceans are running around. They have a hard shell on their top side beneath which they live and move. Everything looks harmonious enough but only up until they start climbing up something or other because sooner or later they end up falling on their "heads." And then they just lie there, their numerous legs gesticulating in the water. It takes a good while before they manage to turn themselves over. And then they start all over again. What in the world kind of animals are they, anyway?

And what about you? What kind are you? You're not a thug, you say, nothing happened, but what makes you think you know what a thug looks like? You think of him as acting this way or that. You convince yourself that they're the kind of people you read about in the newspapers and that you're completely different from them. But isn't that precisely what they all say? What do we know about ourselves when it really comes down to it, or about one another for that matter? You are what you do, and if you're truly honest with yourself, then you know that you sometimes verge on what might be considered the most primitive of the primitive, so who knows, perhaps at this very moment down in a dark basement, let's just try to imagine it for a moment, a young woman is lying, bleeding to death. And that's bound to come to light at some point or other and then you'll be the one everyone's reading about in the newspapers.

But right now you're sauntering around with your girls looking at fish together with a lot of other men who are out with their shared children trying to pass the time on a Sunday … Lark and Raven? Where the hell did they go? They're gone. They were here just a minute ago.

I walk back through the glass pipe where sharks and rays are swimming above me, walk into the blue-cold area with northern lakes and oceans. They aren't there, either. I half run into the cafeteria where the line is very long. I take the steps up to the red zone where we were a moment ago and catch sight of them. Lark is busy pointing something out to Raven. She's pointing at one of those ugly crustaceans that's once again struggling to turn over. It isn't going too well.

is my code, I know it is, but that's not helping me much because it won't work. It's Sunday and Annika thought it would actually be a good idea if I went to the SOL building and worked a little on the speech. Especially if I also had the car washed now that I was going out anyway. I agree to do it even though it's really her and her girlfriends who dirtied it on their excursion yesterday.

I look up at the big entrance area made of glass. Centre for Languages and Literature it says in big, square letters. I still try swiping my card one more time. The small light starts to flash. So I punch 2 beep, 2, beep, 1 beep, 8 beep. But the light doesn't turn green like it's supposed to. It turns red.

I decide to try the door on the opposite side of the building. On my way over there I pass a narrow flower bed. I can see the low basement windows situated furthest down the wall. It's somewhere in there that Olga is, if she's still in there.

I go around to the courtyard with all the bicycle stands and the old fruit tree that was allowed to remain standing during the recently completed renovation.

I walk over to the staircase and swipe my card with a quick *swoosh*. The result is the same as before. It doesn't work. This is just so unbelievable, it can't be true. There's a small sticker on the side of the door. indicating that the company Bravida is responsible for the lock system. I get out my telephone and punch in the telephone number on the sticker. Someone's got to be able to help me.

Heeeelllo? someone says on the other end. It sounds like

the person has been sitting there for years just waiting for the telephone to ring and has now been taken by complete surprise when it actually does.

I explain my situation. I say that's it's an emergency, that there are some exam papers on my writing desk that I simply must get ahold of. They have to be corrected by tomorrow.

One moment, he says, whereupon a long time goes by. What in hell is he doing? A teacher calling in on a Sunday to get ahold of his exam papers can't be that unusual a situation.

He's back again. He explains that the problem may be that I haven't renewed my password in a while. Renewed my password? What's that supposed to mean? He explains that for security reasons it has to be renewed every third month. If it isn't, it'll simply stop working.

All right, all right, if that's what you say, but what am I supposed to do now? Can't you let me in so that I can at least get ahold of those damn papers? I mean, isn't there anything you can do, centrally, from where you are? Pause. The voice comes back. He could, perhaps, let me in, but how would that look? If he started letting people in left, right and center?

I park at the bottom of Magistratsvägan

close by the old indoor swimming pool. Who knows, maybe that's precisely the one Malin frequents?

I get out of the car and walk slowly further down the road. The weather is magnificent today. Instead of being here I ought to take the girls and Annika on a trip to the beach or to the forest but, then again, I might as well go through with what I've set out to do.

There it is, the Delphi Dorm. On the right side there's a white modular building complex in three stories with several inner courts that, according to the homepage, has room for approximately 800 students, and according to hitta.se, an Olga Preobraznenskaya is among them. She's the one we need to get ahold of.

I study the gigantic overview map that has a little red dot indicating where I am. Okay, if I am here ●, where is Y54?

I conclude that it must be the building situated furthest away, all the way up to Norra Faladstorget. I enter the area by way of a narrow path with broken tiles. I truly feel that I have entered unknown territory. I don't belong here. There are bicycles everywhere and cardboard boxes that have just been placed out on the sidewalk. It's Sunday, so there are empty bottles lying around from all the parties held by the young people during the weekend.

The building in which Olga lives faces a small, open park area with one of those very popular places with mats and stationary work-out machines for free public use. The weights are fixed to the bars and everything has been bolted down to the ground so that you can't run off with the equipment, should you be so inclined. Four young men are working out together and drinking energy drinks.

At the entrance to Y54 there is an intercom. "Olga Preobraznenskaya" it says, third floor, to the right. Several of the names have been pasted on there with small strips of white paper.

I take a step back and look up at the building. Find the window that must be hers. There are orange curtains and no plants in the windowsill. It looks rather dead, but on the other hand, so do the other windows. Apart from the four guys by the exercise equipment, the area here seems generally dead. It's late Sunday morning.

I shift my focus back to the intercom. Hesitate for a moment, and then press the button next to her name.

I buzz several times but nothing happens.

The four guys have now caught sight of me and are slowly approaching me. They are all holding an energy drink in their hands.

I sense a faint sputtering of unpleasantness in my gut as they come closer and I discover that one of them is Torsten. Of course it's Torsten, because, of course, he must live very close to Olga.

It's time to leave, I realize, so I start walking away from the spot very slowly, without letting on. Not moving too fast, nothing like that, but as soon as I turn the corner I set off in a brief run to increase the distance between us. Then I go back to walking.

Without looking back I criss-cross a lawn toward the car. Taking good, long strides. No one shouts after me and I don't turn my head a single time. Reach Magistratsvägan and sit down in my Volvo. Straighten the rear view mirror and look back. They aren't there. They haven't taken up the pursuit. Taken up the pursuit? And why in the world would they? Have I also become paranoid now? On top of everything else? And another thing: Did Torsten even see that it was me?

It dawns on me that I may have wasted a perfectly good opportunity here. I could have remained standing and asked him whether he knew where Olga was. That way I could have gotten a little clarity on the situation. But what was I to say? I'm this male professor who looks up his female students at their private address. I just wanted to check in on her and see how she was doing. That would never work. That would never work at all. I was so busy getting away from there and it's not until now where I'm sitting in the car that I realize that it seemed as though someone had approached the dark windowsill in her apartment and had looked down at me.

I didn't see that, but I see them now. Torsten and the others. They're coming out from one of the other courtyards and are heading straight for my car.

I turn the key, put the car into gear and quickly drive off.

As I drive homeward through a practically deserted Lund

I sense that I'm having a hard time keeping myself and my reality together. I also sense that my self-confidence is at the lowest that it's ever been. But things can't get any worse, I think to myself as I signal to turn off, almost home. But somehow I also know that they can. Things can always get worse.

When I get out of the car I see Annika behind the kitchen window. She is standing completely still just looking at me. I wave. She doesn't wave back.

I walk through the door. She is standing with both her hands on the kitchen counter, all ten fingers slightly spread as she looks at me sternly .

Hi! I say. She doesn't say hi, but something else instead Where have you been? she asks. At SOL. You know that. I told you that's where I was going. You may have told me, but didn't we agree that you should have the car washed?

It's early that same evening,

and I can hear the water splashing out in the bathroom because the girls are taking a bath together. They are laughing and playing with some plastic animals I bought for them in the Blue Planet museum shop. Annika is sitting on a stool in there and talking on the telephone with her parents, first her father, then her mother. They talk to each other every Sunday.

I myself am standing looking out at the mild June evening where the lilacs are sending pleasant scents through the open yard door.

I have sent Olga a text. I hope you got home safely, I wrote. That was two hours ago and I've been constantly checking my phone ever since. It feels all hot in my hand. I should of course never have done that. Have I gone completely mad? Now I can be more than certain that if something has really happened to her, which of course it hasn't, young people are just always so distracted, I'll be the first one the police and the entire team of investigators will want to thoroughly cross-examine.

The next morning I am pacing back and forth in the main hall

with a cup of coffee in my hand instead of just going down to that basement once and for all to get some clarity on the situation.

I should actually hurry now. It's almost 10 o'clock and I'll be doing a film presentation at a quarter past. I can see that my students have already begun to stream down toward L303b. It's not the best room for showing films, but what can you do? The big auditorium, which is actually a real cinema, is always booked. I have a sneaking suspicion that Film Studies makes shadow bookings for the entire year so that no one else can take advantage of that big white screen which they believe belongs to them and only them, but instead of standing here getting myself worked up over room availability and drinking cold coffee, perhaps I should make my way down to the basement and get this nonsense over with.

I don't know what it is with me, but the more time passes, the harder things seem to get. Perhaps it's because I've started to convince myself that if I actually decide to check and see if she's still there, then she'll be there, but if I don't then everything will be in perfect order and she'll be walking somewhere in Lund hand in hand with Torsten. Those are the two realities which it is up to me to choose between. But I don't want to choose, even though at some point I'll have to.

Perhaps I'm thinking too much about things.

Annika, on the other hand, seems to find everything uncomplicated at the moment. I can sense it. Which in a way irritates me. Because what is there to be so happy about when it comes down to it?

But hold on a minute. There's no reason why I can't wait to go down to the basement until after I've started the film. What's all the rush for, anyway?

And if the child, because that's all she is, doesn't want to respond to my text messages, then that's, quite frankly, entirely up to her.

Babette's Feast

I say, looking out across the big group of students, says so much about Denmark and about the rye-bread-and-beer-soup culture which is so typically Danish. As you've read for today, I say as the projector is warming up, we will encounter the refined French chef, Babette, who has fled from the battles during the Paris Commune and who now finds herself in a miserly landscape in Norway.

I press ▶.

And pay close attention to how the local farmers can't appreciate the choice delicacies she serves up but as soon as the food and good wine have reached their taste buds, they forget their old quarrels, and you'll see how an ecstatic joy starts to spread among them in the warm room as the cows graze outside and the wind blows...

I press ▶ ▶ ▶ but not a damn thing happens.

A messy note taped onto the lectern indicates which wires need to be connected with which and which shouldn't be connected with any of them. It makes absolutely no sense to me.

I start to perspire. First it was my key card, and now this.

Okay, I say. You'll see, we'll be ready in just a minute and then you'll get to see what you came here to see. You'll get to see a film with true depth, let me tell you. For Karen Blixen was a true story teller and Gabriel Axel was a true *auteur*.

They aren't listening, the young people, because they get so easily impatient. That's not what it was like when I was young, we listened to what was said and we did exactly what we were told. If we were asked to underline the word "potatoes" and discuss it with our neighbor, then that's just what we'd do and if we were given a thick book as an assignment to read for the next day, then we'd rush home and read it until dawn, but these days where the students are given just about everything on a silver platter, they have to be entertained in order for them to pay proper attention.

I ask them to arm themselves with the patience they don't possess and rush out the door.

While running down the hall I can already see that Patrick's door is open. It seems I'm lucky, for the building custodian, which is really just a fancy name for janitor, isn't easy to get a hold of, especially when you need him the most.

Hi, I say as I reach the door.

Patrick, who over time has acquired a small potbelly, looks out at me from his elevated position behind some big screens, the function of which are to give a clear signal that the head custodian is in full control of all logistics. Make no mistake, we know the exact location of every single building and room. In front of him on the table is a big mug with the words Malmø FF and a white paper plate with two croissants.

He asks hesitantly what the problem is.

I begin to explain to him as I catch myself starting to stomp my feet impatiently, that I need his help with some technological issues in 303b and if he would be so kind as to come down and assist me for a moment.

He takes a bite from one of his croissants, spilling crumbs everywhere.

Whereupon he answers, to my surprise, that he has been moving tables and chairs after the party since 7 am this morning and he has just sat down for his morning coffee break to catch his breath for a minute which he'd like to do in peace. Furthermore, he's expecting a telephone call, so, sorry, it'll have to wait for 15 minutes, or maybe even longer.

It dawns on me that he may still hold a grudge against me after the episode with the professor of rhetoric.

I tell him that's all well and good that he's taking a break and that he's waiting for a telephone call and all, but I actually don't really give a shit because right now there are up to 80 students sitting in that room and waiting for the film to start and if they don't get their entertainment very soon then God only knows what they might do.

Patrick's mouth drops and remains open.

Then he gets up from his seat behind the screens and for a moment. I think that I have actually succeeded in convincing him and that he'll now go with me to straighten out the technical issues but I am apparently mistaken.

He stops in the doorway. Looks at me with terrified eyes and then he shuts the door right in my face.

There is the sound of a loud click and I realize that he has also locked it.

Two hours later I press my ear against the basement door

because something is going on in there. Are there voices? Is it singing? Low music? The police busy collecting clothing fibres and hair strands and scraping drops of semen from the carpet?

I can picture it all. My heart is beating violently in my chest. What am I going to do now? The film didn't happen. I sent them all home for the summer. I knocked on Patrick's locked door a few times to no avail before giving up. I could hear him talking on the phone in there.

Per-Erik shows up at the other end of the hallway on his way toward me. He is a professor in comparative literature and has a Danish surname and has always made a big deal over the fact that his grandfather was Danish and that he and I therefore should stick together.

He's all right but tends to talk a lot so I take out my cell phone and pretend to be having a conversation. In that way we can make do with just nodding to one another as he passes me by.

I go back to listening at the door once he's disappeared. Yes, it's clear. Someone's in there. I have no idea what's going on. I push down the door handle. It's not locked.

A man is on his knees with his hands on his thighs. He has black hair on his knuckles. He's Muslim and is in the middle of saying his prayers. The room is being used for the exact purpose for which it was designated and that is all well and good.

He has placed his brown sandals on the small colorful mat by the door. There is also some sort of headwear.

The whole room stinks of his extremely smelly feet.

He leans forward in the direction of Mecca and starts chanting something incomprehensible and then gets back up on his knees. And he goes on and on like that. For a very long time. He doesn't register me.

I catch myself getting annoyed with him. Leave. This is a university, not a house of prayer. But Allah be praised that Olga's corpse isn't lying here rotting.

That same evening Annika and I are at a Restaurant called Mediterranean in the middle of Lund

which is, for good reason, famous for its excellent lamb chops. This is truly a Greek country kitchen of the most genuine kind where the owner Vassilis Kourkakis is eager to lend a hand himself and spread good atmosphere among the tables. However, he doesn't get very far with that tonight. I'm not in the mood for it.

Annika and I are sitting outside under an awning, and it's not that we aren't talking together, we are, but it just never really develops into an actual conversation. We don't really manage to reach each other. We only talk about things that don't actually mean anything. It's not her fault. It's mine. I'm not entirely present.

There hasn't been any activity on Olga's Facebook page for several days now. She hasn't made a single update since that Friday when I took her down into the basement. I take that to be a bad sign. And there's more. I went down to the quiet room once more later in the day and I found some dark stains that could have come from blood. They looked fairly fresh.

Annika smiles at me and takes a sip of her wine. I do the same thing. It would have been easier if the girls had been here, too. Then we could have been preoccupied with them in a way. But they are at the movies with their grandparents and they pestered us so much about being allowed to sleep over at Annika's parents' place that we finally gave in. And I know exactly what that means. It means that it's in the air that we're going to do it tonight, now that we have the whole house to ourselves. But the mood doesn't seem to cooperate. To be honest, I no longer desire Annika. I've felt that way for a long time now, and I realize that that's something that happens to most relationships once the everyday life becomes routine. But unfortunately that's not the only reason. I think she's mousey and dull. I realize that I'm the one who has a problem, that I ought to work with myself when it comes to those things, but it doesn't change anything. I just really don't desire her at all.

I begin to realize that it's this whole story with Olga that's gotten my life to fall apart once and for all. Things aren't packed in any more. There is a real life frog within me, and it isn't the kind that turns into a prince when you kiss it. It's completely indifferent to good morals and the right kind of truly valuable human relationships.

By the way, about my birthday, Annika says. Yes, what about it? I ask as I scoop up the last lamb chop from my plate and start eating it with my fingers.

Have you gotten ahold of a tent? she asks.

No, not yet. I can tell that she's disappointed. But I've made a few phone calls, I lie. Why are you asking about that?

Because we should probably expect more people to come than we initially calculated.

What does that mean? How many are we talking about, anyway?

Probably about 55.

55? I say, putting the lamb chop back down on my plate. But we can't be entirely sure that they'll all come, right?

Annika is standing in the darkness in

the living room of our gingerbread house, undressing herself. I myself am out in the garden trying to envision how the big tent that will be needed is going to be raised. There just isn't enough room for it. Not if there are 55 people coming.

If you stretch your imagination a little, then maybe, and if the tent can cover a small part of the terrace, but it might not be able to stand so stable, then.

No, the tent won't fit here. Denmark, on the other hand, can fit into Sweden ten times if we look at their dimensions. And ten times is quite a lot. It's quite something, David once said to me teasingly. It took a few months, or maybe even more, before I found an appropriate response. After all, it's not for nothing that I'm a professor of Danish. I told him that that really depends on how you choose to look at it because you'd have to include Greenland, the world's biggest island, in your calculations. Greenland is part of the Danish kingdom, in which case the dimensions are drastically altered. We're talking 2.2 million perfectly good Danish square meters and from that point of view Sweden suddenly doesn't look quite as impressive, my fine friend.

Annika is calling me. I empty my wine glass. She's almost naked. Except for the lingerie that I bought her for Christmas quite a few years ago. It still fits her nicely. She stands there a little limp, her arms hanging down at her sides. I almost feel sorry for her. She is offering herself to me, that's clear, but she doesn't appeal to me. She really just doesn't.

She approaches me, squats in front of me, unzips my

pants with big movements, slips her hand through the fly and takes it out. She looks up at me.

This is pathetic.

After she's tried to rub me to an erection for awhile, I am filled with a tenderness I haven't felt for a long time. I take her by the shoulders and lift her to her feet. She looks at me quizzically. I gently kiss her on her lips.

I love you, Annika, I say. I really love you, I repeat, and right at that very moment, I really mean it.

(Beware of the Dog)

6

We're having a meeting
about having a meeting

as we do every Thursday. This is the last one before summer vacation and an item emerged today under "miscellaneous business" that I hadn't seen coming. Britta brings it up and it has to do with Patrick, the head custodian and how he's faring. Because it turns out he's actually not faring well at all at the moment. He feels offended, which was triggered by the little clash I had with him on Monday. Britta says that she therefore wants to know exactly what transpired in his office that day.

I say it like it is, that I was in a real fix that particular morning and that I got mad at him because he preferred to sit around and eat pastry rather than do his job and help me.

I see, she says, looking at me above the frame of her spectacles. Her jaw looks strong and she comes across, as she always does, as frighteningly efficient.

But, as I said before, he took offence, Britta says, and to such a degree that he has had to call in sick.

I'm sorry to hear that.

From what I understand, you called him an idiot, is that correct?

I answer, in accordance with the truth, that that may very well be true, that I called him an idiot, but it's worth mentioning that I had approximately 80 students who lost their chance to watch a film because Patrick preferred eating cake to doing his job.

I look around the room in hope of getting some sympathy but the looks I receive are full of not just indignation, but also of the pleasure that follows in the aftermath of such indignation.

In other words, you don't deny having called him an idiot? Britta maintains.

No, I guess I don't.

Idiot, that's not the kind of tone we use around here. We simply don't speak to one another in that way. To be perfectly frank, your behavior is simply unacceptable.

I look at David and Christer. I wouldn't mind a little help here from their end, but I'm not getting any. They're both busy looking out the window.

Well, then I'll just have to not do that, I say. I sense that I don't really have the energy for this confrontation even though I feel that I'm the one who's being unfairly treated.

It is, of course, good, that you yourself can see that you were at fault here, Britta says. From what I understand, you have quite a temper.

Nevertheless, she continues with a look indicating that the crucial part is about to come up, we have concluded that an apology is in order.

An apology?

If you don't want the case to become further complicated, then that's what you need to do.

Britta can certainly get right to the point when she wants to. You've got to give her that. Malin, who is always flashing her breasts at the swimming pools, nods demonstratively.

If it suits all parties, I suggest that we all meet at my office on June 14th at 1 pm.

Okay, I manage to say. I don't know what else to say.

And once you have personally made your apology to Patrick, Britta continues, then he will be willing to put this whole case behind him and we can all move on and go on summer vacation. I think we all need that.

Okay then, I guess, I begin, but it's as though that's the straw that breaks the camel's back, because this is just too much for me to handle on top of everything else. Do you know what's wrong with Sweden? I hear myself say without knowing where I'm going with it.

They all look at me in dismay.

I'll tell you what's wrong with Sweden I continue, and then I blurt out a whole bunch of stuff that doesn't belong anywhere and which I don't really want to say at all. I say that the inhabitants of this country of Sweden have managed to become so fragile and lesbian and handicapped and genderless and dull and hostile to life's pleasures that it's practically unbearable. It almost makes you want to cry. I'm completely unstoppable at this point and before I leave the room I also manage to say that Sweden needs to be flushed down the toilet bowl.

Sweden needs to be flushed down the toilet bowl.

Did I really say that? Yes, I did, and I also said that Sweden could at times be a nauseating, annoying trial on one's nerves.

After having cooled down a little, I'm better able to see that I may have gone too far. I don't really mean it. That is to say: I only mean it a little. I actually like Scandinavia's only modern industrial country with its big forests and deep lakes. Sweden has so much to offer.

But it's too late now. My hand is practically shaking as I drink from my cup. I've gone downtown and am sitting at Espresso House where I've bought a cup of hot chocolate with whipped cream and am now finding myself between coarsely woven flax bags hanging from the walls and a poster of a smiling fair trade farmer in a checkered shirt who looks like the guy you never befriended in some foreign land.

But the guy I never befriended only exists on the poster. Here at Espresso House I'm surrounded by students. It's teeming with students, which is why there are so many cafés, hairdressers, and bicycle shops in Lund.

I suddenly feel like calling Annika and talking with her but she's at a conference and won't be back until tonight.

I don't know whether it is my true, sick inner self that has come to light as an expression of what I've always been, or whether it's something which the reality in which I find myself has forced up to the surface. At any rate, I know that I have now definitively opened the door to my own downfall. There is no way back. Said is said and done is done.

Zlatan. I am reminded of Zlatan. Sweden has Zlatan. You've got to give them that. I'm sure there are those who'd say that Zlatan isn't Sweden and that they are only selecting him for the national soccer team and use him in Volvo commercials to buy themselves some of that wildness that can no longer be found anywhere else. Look, it's Zlatan, not only is he a Swede but he's also the result of Sweden's wonderful integration policy.

But enough about Zlatan. How am I ever going to get out of this hellish mess I've gotten myself into?

(This Area under Video Surveillance)

There she is, Annika,

on the platform between track five and six. In the middle of a group of colleagues. They're busy saying good-bye and agreeing with each other that this was a seminar that truly yielded something and which gave them something not only on a professional level, but on a personal level as well.

I have been under the impression that they had a lot on the agenda and that they haven't had time for all that many breaks. When I spoke with Annika on the phone last night, I got the clear sense that for her it was just a matter of getting off the phone as quickly as possible so that she could get back and partake in the activities.

I stay in the background. I'm standing on Station Square a few platforms away and observe them. We always pick each other up at the rear side of the building.

Now they are all going their separate ways. Or rather, Annika remains standing a little while longer together with a tall man with blond hair. An SJ-train passing through from Stockholm to Malmø and that doesn't stop in Lund disrupts my field of vision. When the long train has finally disappeared Annika and the tall blond man are busy going each in their own direction.

I rush back to the parking lot and wait for her there.

When a little while later we're sitting in the car on our way home, I ask her whether it was a good conference.

She says that it was overall a good course, but that it didn't give her quite as much as she had hoped for.

That's how it often is, I answer, and then I ask her who she was saying good-bye to at the station.

She answers that it was Henrik Henriksson whom she's been sharing office space with for the last six months.

I then ask whether he wasn't also the one with whom she planned the internat. That was at least my impression.

Perhaps it was, she says.

Ikea is the capital of Sweden

I write, and cross it out again. I can't seem to find any inspiration, and in just a few days I'll be giving my first lecture at the Association of the North and everything's just out of control.

I'm simply unable to concentrate on anything anymore. Meanwhile, others seem to have no problem with it. Annika has started jogging again, buying new clothes, and consuming large quantities of kiwis.

For a long time I've been wondering like crazy about

what to get Annika for her birthday so today I've driven to Miljøgården just outside of Lund. This is where you go to find the finest in Danish design, Danish design at its best, which is exactly what I'm aiming for. Less won't do. Not only is it timeless, it's also in perfect taste. There are those who are under the impression that Danish design has become kitsch, but I completely disagree with them.

And what do we have here? I say to Lark who has come with me. She likes the scent of new furniture. We're standing in front of Denmark's number one easy chair: The Egg.

I tell Lark that it was introduced to the world when Arne Jacobsen decorated the Royal Hotel in the middle of Copenhagen which resulted in the creation of the two most iconic pieces of furniture in the history of Denmark: The Swan and the Egg. I mention to her that both of them are, of course, direct references to Hans Christian Andersen, because Denmark is and will always be a fairytale land and if, for example, you were to drive along…

I'm interrupted by a salesperson who comes forward and asks if he can be of any help. I tell him that we're just having a look at the chair. He is immediately up on the ball at the prospect of possibly being able to sell an Arne Jakobsen lounge chair from Fritz Hansen. He says it's their battleship. And after having talked about the quality at great length, I want to know how much they'd want for it. Because there's no price tag, as far as I can see. I know that it's expensive, but on the other hand, celebrating one's

40th birthday isn't exactly an everyday occurrence. 40 is particularly special, I explain to Lark. There's no getting around it.

The salesman, who is wearing a blue shirt with a white collar, consults his iPad. He presses a few buttons before coming up with the sum: 65,000.

It's just like you see right here, in leather and aluminum and no footstool, he says.

It is very nice, I say, running the palm of my hand across the round part at the very top of the backrest, but I've been wondering whether fabric might be an option now that the kids aren't so little anymore. I'm not sure, but I'm under the impression that there are more colors to choose from in fabrics.

The original chair was, as a matter of fact in leather, says the salesperson who is wearing a small name tag on his chest. His name is Hjalmar.

That may be, I say, but I don't think it's just a question of colors but also of the furniture that's already in the living room. The various pieces should match one another and be able to communicate with one another.

He has to agree with me on that.

I saw one that was displayed at Vestergaard Møbler in Christianshavn. It was practically light blue.

I haven't come across that color, says Hjalmar.

No, that may be, but it exists and that's probably the sort of thing I had in mind.

But that's of course something I need to look into.

I smile at Lark.

But thanks for your help. I think we need to go home and think about it, then we'll see.

7

It's June 14th,

the birthday is only three days away, and in approximately an hour I am to report to Britta's office if I have any hopes of saving my skin. I've decided to take the rough with the smooth because what else can I really do when it comes down to it? Nothing. There is just no way around having to make the apology that is anticipated at the meeting.

But right now it's a matter of getting that tent from "Lund's Tent Rental" transported home. We've already put the longitudinal plastic cases containing pegs and rods in the trunk so the only thing we pretty much need now is to fasten the tent itself up on the newly washed car's roof rack. Well, "only" is perhaps a little bit of an exaggeration, because the thing weighs a ton. My father-in law and I have been struggling with it for almost half an hour. And even though he clearly isn't lacking in will, his physical stamina isn't what it used to be. That's why I ask whether we should go in and ask someone to lend a hand. We should really also ask for some extra straps with which to fasten it.

That won't be necessary, we'll manage it, he says.

Okay, I say, and we continue. That's his problem then.

And then the rain starts. Warm drops from the sky that feel pleasant at first.

It's raining, my father-in-law says.

Yes, it is.

Through the car window, I can see that the display on my cell phone has lit up on the driver's seat. A message has been received. If I strain my eyes I can actually see that it's from Olga.

It's raining a lot now. My father-in-law is already soaking

wet, his T-shirt, his Fjällrävs pants, and his big beard. As I let go of the tent with one hand, I manage to open the car door with the other and pick up the telephone from the seat.

I'm going to have to take this one, I say, shaking the cell phone in the rain.

Is it Annika? he asks.

I just shake my head.

Olga apologizes for not having answered my messages (there was, in fact, only one) but she hasn't been able to because so much has been going on in her life that she's had to see to. She writes in Swedish.

I can see that my father-in-law is about to sink down on his knees and that his face is slightly red from the strain. He smiles at me as though to say, take your time, everything's under control here.

Olga wants to speak with me. It's important, she writes. She wants to know whether today would be good. She suggests 4 pm. That's in only two hours.

I should be able to make that, I write completely irrationally, not really knowing what I'm thinking of.

So I would like to take the opportunity,

now that we are gathered here at Britta's office, to extend a heartfelt apology for the behavior I displayed on the last day before summer vacation, that is, on the morning of June 3rd when I paid your office a visit, Patrick.

Pause.

It's so out of place.

Patrick is standing next to Britta with his hands folded in front of him. The corners of his mouth are turned downward and his eyes are moist. He looks like he has just had a haircut.

There is also a representative from the union present probably to make sure that everything goes smoothly. He is a small man wearing a blazer that's slightly too big for him. He hasn't said much but has a rather serious look on his face.

Malin is there too. I actually really don't see why she's there, but she is. She doesn't want to miss out on anything.

I would also like to emphasize, I continue, that I am aware of the fact that we, in an academic world, where everyone can't necessarily be friends with everyone, must always strive to behave properly and show the appropriate consideration for one another.

Britta is about to say something but I beat her to the punch.

And I would at the same time like to thank Britta and Malin for having drawn my attention to the injustice I have committed.

Patrick gives his colleagues an insecure glance and it looks as though their smiles are fading somewhat. I will soon be through. I'm in a hurry now anyway. I have to meet Olga in twenty minutes.

The road from here to hell is, as mentioned before, paved with bad excuses and I'm certain that the students who never got the chance to see the film I had planned to show them will go on living blissfully in their ignorance of Gabriel Axel and Blixen and, anyway, what with all the wars and destruction going on in the world it is, of course, a mere trifle, a tiny matter of insignificance that isn't worth spending too much time pondering over and, Patrick, I want you to know that when the day comes when you need someone to back you up, you can rest assured that this won't ever come between us.

Olga pulls out the chair

and sits down.

Hi, she says nonchalantly as she removes her sunglasses and places them on the table.

I catch myself observing her for a moment. The high cheekbones, the green eyes and the white skin that never gets tanned. It's over three weeks ago since I last saw her. To think, I have touched her all over, had my hands up underneath her dress and everything.

Do you want anything? I ask. She shakes her head. I've asked her to meet me at Espresso House. I wasn't going to risk meeting her at the university the way things stand now.

I ask her how she's doing.

Good, under the circumstances, she says.

I don't know how to interpret that answer. I haven't had the chance to prepare myself mentally for this meeting with her. But we're sitting here now and there's nothing that would indicate that I have harmed her in any way.

I don't know where to begin, yet it's really her that's taken the initiative to this meeting. So she should be the one to start off.

I want to apologize for my behavior, I say and continue on the apologetic route that I began in the meeting earlier today. It feels completely natural, as though I could continue on that track for all eternity. Sorry, sorry, sorry.

She looks at me. That's okay she says. I actually don't think we should talk about it.

But I'd like to.

Olga shakes her head.

I'm unsure, I insist, of what exactly happened and I've

really felt very bad about it. Something or other tells me that I may have gone way too far.

I don't mention the fact that at one point I had convinced myself that I had pushed her down off the couch and that she had died as a result. That thought seems completely ridiculous now.

Then she opens her mouth, and I sense that she's somehow pulling herself together and then she says that nothing significant happened, we both got drunk and that she actually understands why I got irritated with her if that was what I meant.

I say that I don't know what I meant. That makes her smile cautiously.

She says that the reason why she hadn't reached out has been because she has been to Russia where her mother has just undergone an operation. They have removed one of her lungs, she says, but the doctors are very optimistic.

But she still smokes, she added, smiling again.

Of course she still smokes. Chain smoking is obligatory in Russia.

I'm sorry to hear that, I answer, but I won't lie. Naturally I feel a small rush of relief run through my body.

What she says explains a lot, if not most if it. Except for the blood. She must be able to clear that up, but I suddenly feel like having a cup of coffee.

I think I'll have a cup of coffee after all, I say, getting to my feet. What about you? She doesn't want any.

I have hardly left the table before she takes out her phone and starts fiddling with it. That irritates me slightly.

I wait in line for an eternity and the rather heavy-set young girl who constantly wipes her hands in her apron gives me a lazy look when it gets to be my turn. I order an Americano and step to the side, continuing my wait. I look toward the direction of our table.

Olga is still fully absorbed in her telephone. What in hell could be so damn important? Her hair is ebony black and shiny. She must have dyed it again. Why did she want to meet at all? What is this all about? She hasn't said anything about that yet.

Then I catch sight of Annika. She's coming through the door. And she's not alone. She is accompanied by the same tall man she said good-bye to at the station. I also recognize his shoulder bag, the strap of which he wears across his chest. He is a slim academic-type with blond curls. The glasses he's wearing resemble mine but they don't suit him very well. Not by a long shot. He's probably every mother-in-law's dream, something which, on the other hand, is completely indisputable.

After a few more seconds Annika catches sight of me, whereupon her lips slide into an insecure smile.

(Ball-Playing Not Allowed in This Area)

This tastes really wonderful,

Annika says that same evening while we are sitting on the bench at the dinner table. She looks at me straight in the eye as she passes the melted butter around.

I have baked white fish in the oven and am pouring sauce on my potatoes before passing the bowl to Lark. Raven has already left the table. She's doing her homework upstairs in her room. I have told Lark that if she has finished eating then she, too, may be excused.

Your mother and I also have something to talk about, I add.

Lark slides off her chair and runs up the stairs.

I shift my focus toward Annika.

He seems very nice, this Henrik, now that I've seen him, I say.

She never got a chance to see Olga who ever so discreetly snuck out the door.

Annika sips her wine and starts explaining that because their collaboration has proven more fruitful than is normally the case, she and Henrik plan to apply for funding for a joint research project. That was what their meeting was about at Espresso House.

Yes, that's what you said, I say, and your chances of getting money should be pretty good since they seem to be fairly generous when it comes to distributing money around at the moment.

Henrik is primarily a veterinarian, Annika confides to me.

Primarily a veterinarian? I can't follow you now.

He is trained as a vet, but ever since he was very young

he's had a weakness for English literature, especially DH Lawrence and Jane Austen.

English literature?

Yes, Henrik has read every book that he could get his hands on by those two authors and several years ago he made a drastic decision. At that point he had just taken over his father's animal hospital, but he sold it and started to study literature.

She pauses for a moment before continuing. That is a decision you have to admire. And on top of that his sense of humor is very refreshing.

Yes, a sense of humor is important, no doubt about that, but what is your research project going to be about?

We're going to examine what kind of birds fly around in Nordic poetry. .

She smiles just at the thought of it.

On the Faro Islands there are, for example, many puffins. In Denmark there are many dovetails, starlings and ducks, while in Norway there are more so-called dippers that prefer to inhabit pure streams with strong currents. In Greenland there really aren't any at all.

I say that that sounds like an exciting project.

Yes, and I have previously worked with flora so I guess it's about time I delve into fauna.

I try to think of something to soften up the mood even more, but nothing comes to mind.

I repeat that I think that it sounds like an interesting project they're working on and I also mention that should they find themselves in need of some knowledge that a seasoned Danish teacher and ethno-geographer like myself can contribute, they shouldn't hesitate to ask.

That's very nice of you but we really already have a good idea of how we're going to tackle it so that won't be necessary, Annika answers as she gets up and starts clearing the table.

Every relationship has their ups and downs

I say to myself as I, a little while later, load the dishwasher. At the moment things are going mostly down. Which is, of course, a shame, now that the big birthday bash is soon coming up, but it'll probably all work out fine in the end. I'm sure it will.

But there's also something else occupying my thoughts. Olga said there was something she wanted to talk with me about but she never got a chance to before Annika showed up together with the literature cum veterinarian Henrik.

I place a white capsule with a blue ball in the middle in the small plastic holder, press the button and close the door. The dishwasher starts with a roar.

I'm still wondering whose blood was on my shirt. It remains a constant mystery. There may be forbidden desires within oneself which should never see the light of day, and even if you don't want to have anything to do with them they are still there. I could contact Olga but I could also not. The latter would probably be the best.

I go up on the terrace roof of my gingerbread house to collect my thoughts

as I have done so many times before. I can see the Øresund Bridge from there. It's a beautiful bridge. A tight and stylistically pure bridge. And it leads to my homeland. Who knows, maybe I'll move back there someday? No one says I have to stay in Sweden forever. A lot can happen in one's life. Suddenly, out of the clear blue, everything might turn upside down. It wouldn't be the first time. Take, for example, literature-cum-vet Henrik. One moment you've got your hand stuck way up a horse's behind, ready to take over your father's clinic, and the next you've got your head buried in a pile of English poetry books.

8

This time it is Olga

who beats me to the punch with an email, but the sun is hitting my display screen and my contact lenses are stinging because I've stopped using my old glasses and I actually don't feel like reading it right now because it's enough already, there's way too much to deal with at this point and the party is just around the corner. It's tonight.

There's also a racket coming from the other side of the fence where my father-in-law is busy. He has procured a small little garden tractor to mow the grass even though it doesn't need to be mowed at all but I'll just have to accept it if I want his help. Which I do. I've said to him that we should soon get going if we ever want to put up that damn tent. The guests will be arriving in four hours. I should get going on it myself, but the girls are busy out on the playground chasing the cat that belongs to the family next door. They're trying to throw some of the water on it which they've managed to collect from the wet surfaces of the playground.

It rained last night. Let's just hope it stays dry tonight.

I am just about to click on the email after all to see what Olga has to say when I suddenly hear my father-in-law shouting for me. He has stopped the tractor. It has something to do with the quince trees.

And let me conclude this, my speech,

by saying that I wish and hope, Annika, that you stay the same and don't change in the least bit, and first and foremost remain the devoted mother you've always been to our two wonderful daughters, Lark and Raven, who, like two beautiful birds, flew out of you when you were still a young woman.

It gets quiet for a moment after I've said the last words and I am perfectly aware of the fact that the image those words have conveyed wasn't exactly the best in the world. But no one can say that I haven't been thorough in my choice of topics from my depiction of Annika's life. I have also remembered to thank her parents for all their efforts on our journey up until today.

Let's make a toast, I conclude as I gesture that it's time for everyone to stand up.

It's quite impressive that we have enough space for 62 people under the roof of the tent, but we do, in fact. It also has to do with the fact that my father-in-law, it later became apparent, had been busy felling the two quince trees which was why he had been shouting at me. But that's okay because they were situated awkwardly anyway.

We've been lucky with the weather, at one point rain and wind had been in the forecast, but we seem to have escaped that. We've also been lucky with the food. In fact, we've been lucky overall with most everything.

I hear the sound of the applause and empty my glass, placing it a bit too hard on the table.

I leave my seat and walk over to the two chefs that are busy packing everything down. They've already carried most of their gear back to the car. I tell them that the paella which they prepared in two big steel dishes above the open fire as they stirred it with big wooden spoons was excellent. It gave a sense of seeing something genuine, as opposed to just getting the food delivered in big heating cupboards. This was truly something completely different. They both agree with me.

However, I say to them, you were a bit stingy when it came to certain ingredients, like the shrimp, for example, but we'll leave it at that. We were generally pretty satisfied.

They quickly pack the rest in the car and drive off.

I go back to the table and pour myself another big glass of wine. This time it's red. We've bought plenty of red, white, and rosé in jugs. I've already had quite a lot of all three, but, then again, it's not every day that your wife turns 40.

I decide to put on a little music, there has to be music. I've prepared a playlist full of Annika's favorite musicians. Bo Kasper's Orchestra and Lisa Ekdahl. I've also included a few little Danish surprises like Anne Linnet, Love Shop, Marie Key and of course, the one and only Kim Larsen's "Kvinde min" ("My Woman").

I decide that we should start out with "Kvinde min." Of course, what else? It'll be great. How could it not be?

At the table, I'm sitting next to the short-legged Kamilla

who is Annika's best friend. She is the principal of a high school in Eslöv and she's spent most of her adult life producing children. She's on her fifth one now, but there may yet be more to come. Her husband is nothing but a small shrimp of an engineer who works in the chemistry industry.

She asks me how things are at work and what it is I actually work with.

I tell her things are good, for while others are preoccupied with the birds and trees of literature, I find more challenge and excitement in pursuing supermarkets, parking garages and train stations stained with old pieces of chewing gum on the platforms, and even though I realize you can't quite follow me right now, I want to let you in on a little something, Kamilla, and that is that Sweden is filled with those kinds of lamentable places, take for example, Segel's Torg and those huge chunks of concrete that have been placed by Folkhemmet in Stockholm.

But Sweden has so much to offer, I know, I continue after having emptied my third glass.

By the way, do you know what Sweden has to offer that Denmark doesn't have? I ask her, to which I answer before she has a chance to say anything: Good neighbors.

Kamilla looks at me sternly. The others sitting around the table, and who must have heard my little joke, aren't laughing either.

Yes, well, humor hasn't exactly ever been Sweden's strongest point, something which I've discovered by now, but hell, the only fun you have is damn well the fun you create for yourself.

Kamilla resembles Malin at work a lot when she has that look. The gift she gave wasn't worth mentioning, either. A Japanese porcelain bowl, rectangular. On a fortieth birthday!

I keep somewhat of an eye on Annika

because it is, after all, her party. She's sitting at the table situated furthest away in the garden together with her colleagues. She is wearing a flowery dress and a white, practically see-through cardigan. She's sitting on the gift that I gave her so I think she's happier with my present than she initially expressed.

After much pondering, I decided to pass up on Danish design. I concluded that things don't have to be so materialistic all the time so instead I bought her a wicker chair made from old plastic bags. It was made by some design students in Malmø, so in that way I'm also supporting the use of cambium. I also managed to weave something about the chair into my speech.

But forget the gift. She's wearing an old hat which she must have borrowed from someone or other. I don't think it suits her. In fact, it doesn't suit her at all, she really should take it off.

I decide that I ought to tell her so I get up from the table to do it, but on my way I catch sight of a figure on the playground through the hole in the fence and the vision rushes through me like a small, unpleasant chill. It's Olga standing out there, or sitting, rather, because she's sitting on one of the swings in the twilight, her legs kicking underneath her, like you see with small children. Lark and Raven, for example. when they feel very hurt. She is wearing white rubber boots.

I have to deal with this.

This won't do at all. I'll simply have to ask her to scram because she can't just come here and ruin everything, she won't get away with that, and I walk past Annika and her ugly hat and continue out through the fence. Luckily no one notices me. What am I to do with her now?

Come, come over here!, I say to Olga, and she does as I say, jumping off the swing and following me to the other side of the playhouse where, true enough, the bench on which I had planned we could sit is situated, but we can't, because the neighbor's cat is standing there with its stiff legs, arching its back.

It's humongous. They feed it way too much. They ought to eat some of the food they give it themselves because they're all very skinny.

We walk a little further off, a good distance along the bicycle path and I say to Olga that she can't just show up like that and that she must be able to understand that.

She doesn't answer. Looks up at me with her head askew as she brushes away some hair from her forehead. Has she dyed it again? I really think it's getting to be too much and if she's used that cheap crap that they sell in Russia, there's a good chance that her hair will end up smelling like ammonia or kerosene.

What do you want? What are you doing here? I continue when she still doesn't say anything.

I hear laughter coming from the party. I'm terrified that someone's going to catch sight of us from the yard.

She asks why I haven't answered her email and I say that as she herself can see, if she has eyes that is, well, I've got quite a bit on my plate right now.

She wants to know what I think of her idea. That's why she's come. She has to know before she does anything.

I don't know what she's talking about, what it is she has to "do", because I haven't read that damn email, but I don't really feel that I can admit that, so I say it's best if she goes first.

She starts by saying a whole lot of things very quickly, but from what I can gather from what is coming out of her mouth which, to be honest, sounds mostly Russian, Torsten has suggested that they get engaged and move to London together and look for work.

Well, I didn't see that coming, I begin, and for a moment I feel slightly disoriented, but only for a moment, because suddenly I see an opportunity that will, once and for all, get rid of all the worries this whole thing has caused me, so I say that that sounds like a good solution. Both to get engaged and go to England.

Before she has the chance to answer me, I give her a quick hug and say that naturally in a situation like this I'm willing to put my own needs and egocentric interests aside, sweep them away, and let youth blossom.

I give her another hug and can't help but notice that her hair doesn't smell like ammonia at all. It smells like vanilla and seems soft and fine.

She gets on her bike, which she has apparently parked at Netto Supermarket, which also happens to be the place in Sweden where I can buy my Stryhns Danish liver paté. But before she bikes off and the scent of vanilla is still lingering in my nose, I hold on to her luggage carrier for a brief moment and tell her that should she at some point in the future, after all one never knows in life, find that she would like to take up her assignment again, then I'll be the man ready to take it on. She should never be in doubt about that.

But get home safely and have a safe trip to London, I conclude, and let her bike away.

I rush back through the fence

and lift one of the cases of wine. It's half full, but it's red, and it would have been nicer to have some rosé- It's the rosé that I want, so I take my time strolling around a little in search of it and when I manage to find what I'm looking for, I fill the glass to the brim, because if I can't spoil myself on a night like this, when could I do it then? Just when I thought that my entire life was about to be shattered to pieces, I'm told that all my problems will soon be boarding a plane bound for England. That's got to be celebrated.

I put on some music and turn up the volume because now it's time to really get the party going. I get a hold of Kamilla and try to pull her onto the dance floor but she resists.

Somebody's got to be the first, I say, as I take a couple of crazy steps to "Du er så smuk og dejlige." This is just so fun.

Okay, so maybe Kamilla, that bitter tart, doesn't want to dance but who cares, because all things considered my first dance should really be with the birthday girl. She's my wife and that needs to be celebrated, too.

If I can find her, that is. Where is Annika? Oh, she's standing there in the kitchen.

She's talking on the phone and has a serious look on her face. Which she shouldn't have, because the juices are rising in me like they do in summertime in the quince trees, which we don't have anymore because my father-in-law cut them down but who cares? We've got each other.

She's so beautiful, even though she's still wearing that hat.

I point and gesticulate that she's wanted on the lawn's

provisional dance floor but she waves me away. Then I empty my glass and dance on my own out into the yard even though I can't fathom how there could possibly be any important phone calls on a night like this, but apparently there can. Well, that's just the way it is.

The party is really under way now and

there are more people out dancing. I'd like to join them but my tongue has swollen up and is filling my whole mouth because I've been pouring out the wine for the guests, myself, and that guy Henrik who's just arrived.

I have to take a pee, because what comes in has to go out, so I go into the living room and continue into the hallway to find the guest toilet occupied.

Well, then, we'll just have to go upstairs then, won't we, and use the bathroom instead. No problem in that. On my way up the stairs I almost fall out of the big window facing the street but I quickly regain my balance. Everything's spinning around.

Damn it! Someone's also relieving themselves in there as well. I go out into the yard again and look for Annika. I haven't seen her for awhile. I've got to find her. But first I've got to pee so I go back inside. Both bathrooms are still occupied.

I wait for a minute in front of the bathroom door on the second floor, knock, but no one answers. That's not right, on the other hand, there's isn't anything I can do about it.

Instead I continue all the way up to the third floor and go out on the rooftop patio where a pleasant breeze blows in my face.

I can see the lights on the Øresund Bridge, flashing red and white, so that the airplanes that are on their way to London, for example, won't fly into the bridge piers, but I've got to piss so terribly bad at this point that my bladder is on the verge of exploding, so I climb across the railing and walk out onto the flat, asphalt tiles, unzip my pants and let the water flow in wonderful, relieving streams.

I look down at the yard where many people are dancing except for Kamilla, who's standing staring up at me with eyes as big as tea cups as the pool of urine before me continues to grow bigger and I even see some of it running along the gable and dripping down into the lawn.

9

I could perhaps have restrained myself a little

but on the other hand, it's not every day that your wife turns 40. I remember going back inside from the roof after having waved at the eternally angry Kamilla, but since I didn't have a great urge to go back down to the yard I ended up instead in the laundry room where I must have fallen asleep under a pile of laundry.

I look around in the yard. There's quite a big job left for us today because there are still scraps of food on the paper plates and wine in the plastic cups. The tent also needs to be taken down and returned today. I assume that my father-in-law will come and help me with that. I have no recollection of when my in-laws went home. We'll have to see. There are also some blue boxes with baking tins and silver platters that have to be returned to the caterer. Some of the tables and folding chairs were borrowed from the neighbor.

I find a garbage bag and start filling it with garbage. You've got to start somewhere.

I know that my behavior wasn't too impressive last night, and I could have done without my little stunt on the roof. But...

There she is, in the kitchen. The birthday girl with her heavy breasts under her white t-shirt. What's she doing? She's looking out here, so I get back to work, start folding up the chairs and piling them up by the garden shed.

She's coming out to me now. Her legs and toes are bare. Almost like a little flower child.

Hi, I say, but I continue folding the chairs.

It went well yesterday, I say, the food was good and, by the way I promised your friend Kamilla that I would give her the chef's number. It'll be their turn next year, with Martin.

Annika nods. She is standing looking out through the hole in the fence.

She still doesn't say anything and, yes, of course Kamilla couldn't keep her mouth shut.

What's done is done and we can't go around being angry with one another for all eternity. We've got to move on like the adults we are. I'm sure we'll be telling our grandchildren about it someday. That time when Grandpa stole the show at Grandma's fortieth birthday party.

I tell her that I'm really starting to look forward to the trip to Bulgaria. We'll get our own swimming pool for the girls and should we get the urge for a cup of coffee in the middle of the night we can get it free of charge in the cafe that's open 24/7. That's what you call *all- inclusive*.

I don't think I'll be wanting to go to Bulgaria after all, she says.

I don't understand what she means and I definitely don't like the way she says it.

Bulgaria isn't as bad as it's reputation, I insist, but we can also go somewhere else naturally. For example, I think we might find a special offer for Lalandia if we avoid the Danish summer season.

She shakes her head. I don't think it makes much difference where we go on vacation and it doesn't have anything to do with you. I just think I'm at a place in my life … pause … where I'm not so sure what I want anymore.

Does this have something to do with that guy Henrik Henriksson? I ask.

A new pause.

Unfortunately, that can't be entirely ruled out. But it's too early to say now.

Okay.

It's as though something is unleashed inside of my head and I take the black plastic bag and throw napkins, plastic forks and other garbage into it, and even though it might not be the same thing as looking deep down into Kierkegaard's abyss, while walking along the tables, it feels as though I'm throwing myself into the garbage bag which, by the way, has a hole in it.

ROBERT ZOLA CHRISTENSEN Ph.D., has written more than 30 books in both non-fiction and fiction (novels, crime fiction, children books). His works have been translated into several languages, including German, French, Serbian, Russian and Swedish. His latest novel, *No Balloons* (2017), explores the different lifestyles in Scandinavia, political correctness and the role of man today. Originally from Denmark, Robert Zola Christensen is currently an Associate Professor at Lund University in Sweden.

NINA SOKOL is a poet and translator in the midst of translating novels, short stories. plays and poems by Danish writers. She was a grant poet-in-residence at The Vermont Studio Center in 2011. She has received several grants from the Danish Art's Council to translate plays, including a play written by the fairy tale writer H.C. Andersen which was published by the journal "InTranslation." She has also translated an excerpt from one of the winning novels of last year›s EU Prize for Literature (Danish, 2016) as well as translated such authors Niviaq Korneliussen and Bjørn Rasmussen. Her own poems have appeared in American journals, including *Miller's Pond* and the *Hiram Poetry Review* and a collection was published by Lapwing Publications in Belfast, Ireland (2015).